breath catching in her tⁱ.... ..e dipped his head towards her.

Her eyes fluttered shut as he pressed his lips to hers, their gentle pressure soon building to the passionate exchange she'd been waiting for.

He cupped the curve of her backside and pulled her closer, fitting their bodies perfectly together. Lola heard herself moan and felt her hand slide from the door handle, all thoughts of leaving this corridor vanishing by the second. Pinned in place by his hands and lips, she'd never felt so wanted... so safe.

Lola all but slid to the floor when he let go of her.

'For the record, when we're both ready to take the next step you will have my *full* attention.'

His husky-voiced promise sent goosebumps over Lola's skin once more. If this was Henri when he was distracted, Lola wasn't sure she would survive him at full strength. Although she'd be happy to die trying.

On that thought, Henri took her hand and kissed it like a true gentleman. Only the wink as he left her gave away that devilish side she knew lurked within.

Lola sigh... ...bedroom, thoroughly... ...utely no chance...

…n't believe my dream of becoming a Mills and …n® author has finally come true! Thank you for …ying my debut novel and being part of it.

French Fling to Forever sprang to life from one small item—a pink stethoscope. I wanted my heroine to be a real girlie girl, but one so emotionally scarred she can't see her own beauty. Bullying has become such a serious issue I thought it was important to highlight the long-term damage it can cause. Although I was lucky enough never to endure the cruelty Lola endured as a teenager, I definitely share some of her insecurities.

This is the story of her strength, and the fight back against her childhood tormentors.

Of course a hot Medical Romance™ wouldn't be complete without a sexy doctor, and a brooding French registrar is the perfect man to help Lola move on from the past. I hope you'll love Henri as much as I do…*swoon*!

If you would like to get in touch you can reach me on Twitter, @karinbaine1, or on Facebook: www.facebook.com/KarinBaineAuthor

Enjoy!

Karin xx

Karin Baine lives in Northern Ireland with her husband, two sons, and her out-of-control notebook collection. Her mother and grandmother's vast collection of books inspired her love of reading and her dream of becoming a Harlequin Mills & Boon® author. It wasn't until she joined her critical group, UCW, that she started to believe she could actually write—and only her husband's support has enabled her to pursue it. At least now she can tell people she has a *proper* job!

French Fling to Forever
**is Karin Baine's debut title
for Mills & Boon® Medical Romance™!**

For Mum and Granny Meta.
I miss you both every day. xx

This book would never have happened without the
love and support of my husband George and our boys.
A mention also to the rest of the family, who have
put up with my writer/hermit craziness for years!

I would need another book to list all those who
helped me on this journey, but know I appreciate each
and every one of you. Especially Michelle Handyside,
who has answered my endless medical questions, and
Julia Broadbooks, who has talked me down
from the ledge on many, many occasions.

CHAPTER ONE

LOLA TOOK A sip of sweet tea and did her best to blank out the anxieties vying for space in her head. *Am I up to the job? Can I cope with making life-or-death decisions? Where are the toilets?*

Over the rim of her cup she watched a sea of blue scrubs fill up the hospital canteen. The laughter and general chatter of her new colleagues did little to comfort her. They were so at ease, confident in their surroundings. She was sure she was the only first-year doctor here with knots in her stomach. Despite her promise to herself that her placement here in the Belfast Community Hospital would be another step towards independence, she was tempted to run.

Until recently she'd always had her brothers close by, to reassure her and take her by the hand when she needed it. It had been her idea to leave home once she'd graduated from medical school, although she wasn't sure if moving across the city to flat-share with her best friend counted as a particularly bold move.

Right now she needed one of those warm bear hugs only big brothers could give. This sense of isolation wasn't alien to her, but it was still as daunting as it had been at fifteen, when her whole world had fallen apart. Even now, almost ten years later, Lola couldn't shake off the paranoia that everyone was watching her and judging her and that at some point she'd be made to pay for being different.

She jumped as the first dramatic chords of her mobile phone's ringtone blared from her pocket and jolted her back from her nightmarish thoughts. It wouldn't do for her to get lost in those dark thoughts of pain and humiliation when she was due for her induction into the emergency department in fifteen minutes.

She was sure every pair of eyes in the room swivelled towards her as her clammy hands fumbled to retrieve the phone.

'Hello, sis.'

Instead of turning it off, she'd managed to accept a call from the eldest of her three big brothers. That protective older sibling intuition was uncanny.

'Er...hi, Jake.'

She would have given a sigh of relief if it hadn't have been for the 'No Mobile Phones' signs screaming at her from the walls. If she didn't take the call now the rest of the family would surely hound her all day, since it was they who'd insisted she carry this blasted thing. Tea abandoned, she hurried out into the corridor to avoid further disapproving stares.

'How's it going?' Jake unknowingly provided the virtual arm around her shoulders that told her she wasn't on her own.

'I haven't started yet. I'll phone you when I get home.' Tears pricked Lola's eyes that her siblings knew her well enough to pre-empt her anxiety in an unfamiliar environment. Despite their sometimes overzealous interest in her personal life, she didn't know what she would do without them.

'I'm in the car park. I've got something for you.'

Jake sounded so pleased with himself Lola didn't have

the heart to snub him. Besides, an *actual* hug would surely set her up for the rest of the day.

'In that case I'll see you in a couple of minutes.'

This time she did hang up, and then raced through the gleaming white corridors to meet him, the flat rubber soles of her shoes squeaking on the polished hospital floors.

Jake stood waiting for her in the ambulance bay, his striking features attracting the attention of every passing female. All three of her brothers resembled their father with their swarthy appearance, whilst she was the image of her blonde-haired, green-eyed mother. Sometimes she believed that was the reason her father had distanced himself from her. She was a painful reminder of the woman who'd walked out on him and left him to raise four children alone.

'I came to wish you good luck.'

Jake pulled her into his arms, only releasing her when she was sure she could hear ribs cracking.

He thrust a crumpled parcel into her hands. 'And I got you this.'

'Thank you.'

She ripped off the tatty wrapping to reveal a shiny new stethoscope. The thoughtfulness couldn't fail to make her smile. Although she didn't receive much support from either of her parents, with her mother AWOL and her father more concerned about himself, her brothers more than made up for it.

'We made sure we got you a pink one—just in case.' Jake grinned at the family joke.

In order to keep her brothers from pinching her stuff when they were growing up, Lola had learned at an early age to mark her belongings in boy-proof colours.

'Thank you. It's lovely, Jake. But I really have to run. I don't want to stuff things up on the first day.' She gave him a peck on the cheek and slung the gift around her neck.

'No problem. You've got this.'

Another lung-squeezing embrace emphasised his complete support, but Lola was forced to wriggle away as time marched on. She said her goodbyes and waved him off, waiting until he was out of sight before she started running again.

Out of breath, she slid to a halt behind the group already assembled in A&E.

'How nice of you to join us.'

The cutting French accent of her new superior called to her above the heads of her colleagues. She'd heard tales of all the newbies falling for the Gallic registrar and she could see why. Henri Benoit was the stereotypical tall, dark and handsome dreamboat. It was as well Lola had sworn off men prettier than her, or she'd be devastated on a personal level as well as a professional one at starting off on the wrong foot with him.

'Sorry. My brother wanted to wish me good luck.'

Even to herself she sounded like a five-year-old on her first day at big school. Lola whipped the stethoscope from around her neck and wrung it between her hands. The shine of her gift had been dulled under the scorn of her superior.

'Well, Dr—' he scanned her staff pass '—Dr Roberts. In future could you leave your personal life outside the hospital doors?'

'It won't happen again.' Marking a target on her forehead was the last thing a self-confessed wallflower wanted.

'*Bien*. Now that we're all here I will show you where everything is before we let you loose into the big wide world.'

The use of Benoit's mother tongue didn't make him any less intimidating to Lola, but she could almost see the cartoon love hearts in the eyes of the other new female recruit standing next to her. Even the distinctly masculine members of the group were hanging on to his every word.

In different circumstances Lola too might have sighed at the sexy sound of a real live Frenchman instead of the usual Belfast brogue, but as far as she was concerned a scolding couldn't be considered romantic in any language.

Thankfully the heat was off Lola as the registrar took the lead on a whistlestop tour of the department, with most of his eager new staff members nipping at his heels. All except one thoroughly chastened recruit, who hung back and did her best to fade into obscurity.

'This is the resus room and monitoring station. These are the rooms for the walk-in patients...'

Lola did her best to absorb all the information he shot at them. He didn't seem the type to repeat himself, and she wouldn't draw any further attention to herself by asking questions. The cursed gift she had for bringing out the worst in attractive men always resulted in the highlighting of her own inadequacies.

One of these days she would coast through life like everyone else apparently did, without worrying about how she looked to those around her. But for now those cruel voices still whispered in her ear, sneering at her appearance, telling her she wasn't good enough to be here.

Lost in her own thoughts, she drifted into the hub of A&E behind her colleagues. As they attended the bedside of an elderly man Lola suddenly became all too aware that everyone was watching her with expectation. This time she definitely wasn't imagining it. Henri Benoit folded his arms across his chest and raised an eyebrow, clearly waiting for something from her.

Breath caught in Lola's throat and she stared back blankly, wondering what it was she'd done wrong this time.

'*Excusez moi* for interrupting your daydream, Doctor. This patient needs bloods to be taken and I was asking if you would kindly oblige.'

This second dressing down from him was well deserved. She'd let her mind drift from the present into the all-consuming memories of the past.

There was no way she'd ever make a success of her medical career if she couldn't get a handle on her personal issues. Something told her Dr Benoit wouldn't wait around for her to get with the programme, and she owed it to the patients to focus on their problems instead of her own.

With sweaty palms and jelly legs, Lola stepped out of her corner. 'Sir, I'm just going to take some blood.'

Following procedure, she kept the patient informed of her intentions as she approached the bed, trying to keep the tremor in her voice at bay. There was no place for uncertainty in the frantic pace of Accident and Emergency, and she would need an air of authority if she hoped to gain any respect around here. Any wavering in her confidence would only serve to alarm those under her care.

Unfortunately, nerves appeared to have completely got the better of her.

'Sorry, I can't seem to find a suitable vein…' A warm flush infused her whole body as she tapped the patient's arm and attempted to insert the needle a second and a third time.

'One of the key things to remember in these early days is to ask for help when it's needed and not let a patient suffer for the sake of your ego. I'll take over from here.'

Every one of Lola's fears were realised as the registrar used her as an example to the rest of the group of how *not* to be a doctor. The nodding dogs were probably grateful they weren't the ones under the microscope.

Henri Benoit's hand brushed hers when he took the needle from her and the rolling in Lola's stomach reached a crescendo. She backed away for some breathing space, praying she wouldn't embarrass herself any more than she already had by throwing up on his shiny black shoes.

'All done.'

With an ease that Lola envied he finished the job and bagged up the vials for the lab. Once he'd settled the patient again he returned his attention to the group. Although she got the distinct impression he was mainly addressing her.

'The best way to learn is on the job. So get acquainted with the Duty Nurse and assign the patients between you. I'll be around if you need me.'

Lola's shoulders sagged with relief when he left her and her fellow rookies to go it alone.

Naturally, as soon as Dr Suave was out of the picture, she functioned as well as any other member of staff. All further procedures undertaken after that debacle in the morning went as smoothly as they had done in her training. And in any areas where she *did* need some assistance she turned to the nurses for guidance. They were more than helpful, given that she showed respect for their position and experience—which she suspected some new doctors failed to recognise as an asset.

However, she couldn't seem to shake off her disappointment in herself, replaying that monumental cock-up in front of her boss over and over again. At periods during the day she found herself frowning and wincing, which probably looked strange to people not privy to the abject humiliation going on her head.

The end of the day couldn't come quickly enough, and when her shift was over Lola changed into civilian clothes and headed straight for the exit. Her face turned up to the heavens, she let the rain fall and cleanse her weary skin, as though it would somehow wash away everything that had happened back inside those doors.

The umbrella she was eventually forced to put up proved scant protection from the elements. It blew inside out several times as she joined the throng of people heading towards the city centre. She'd agreed to meet Jules, her flatmate, for a night out, and after today she'd earned it.

Most evenings she preferred to study, but Jules had insisted on helping her celebrate her first shift. As an F2, a Foundation Doctor in her second and final year of the training programme between medical school and specialist training, she'd taken it upon herself to instruct Lola in the ways of hospital life inside and outside of the wards.

'We're going to a new place tonight that all the girls in work are talking about. Somewhere you can really let your hair down,' Jules had told her when she'd given her the address of the venue.

For Lola, that was even more terrifying than facing another shift with her French Fancy.

'In burlesque, the emphasis is on the tease rather than the strip.'

Miss Angelique's delicate accent filtered across the dimly lit room to reach the ears of her most reluctant pupil.

In Lola's imagination the exotic sight and sound of the instructor should have transported her to a fabulous Parisian nightclub, where glamour and sophistication went hand in hand. Unfortunately the rumbling sound of buses outside and the accompanying smell of diesel through the open window were a constant reminder that she was stuck in a dingy dancehall in Belfast's city centre.

'When did Northern Ireland become a hotspot for the French populace?' she muttered to Jules, who she now held entirely responsible for her bad mood. Prancing around as some trussed-up, half-dressed version of herself with one of Benoit's countrymen bossing her around wasn't exactly the perfect remedy for all that ailed her. 'Tell me again—why am I doing this?'

'To prevent you from ending up as some sad sack with only her books for company,' Jules said, before her attention wandered back to the stage, where Miss Angelique moved seductively to a teasing big band soundtrack.

'Maybe I like the sound of that.' Lola pouted, and watched enviously as the instructor demonstrated a dance with oversized fluttering fans, never giving away more than a glimpse of the ivory silk corset she wore.

The stunning Frenchwoman projected a confidence in her body she could only dream of. Oh, how she longed to experience that freedom of movement, absent of any self-conscious thought, even for a short while. But owning her own sexuality, regardless of other people's perceptions, was a skill Lola doubted even the fabulous Miss Angelique could teach her.

A pack of savage teenage boys had robbed her of *ever* having any confidence in her own skin. Their laughter still rang in her ears, and she could still see their sneering faces looming above her as they'd held her down and stripped her of her dignity.

She'd been a late bloomer—not helped by the fact that she'd had to wear her brother's secondhand clothes and had sported the same short hairstyle her father gave all his offspring. But it hadn't given anyone the right to call her names, to question her femininity, or demand proof that it existed.

She hated them for the pain they'd caused her—hated the school for not putting an end to the bullying before it had got that far. Most of all she hated herself for letting it happen. A stronger person would have fought them off before they'd exposed and humiliated her. A more attractive girl wouldn't have had to. In the end she'd let herself down, and she was still fighting to make amends.

'Now, ladies, we've already assigned your stage names for this evening, and we need to bring your alter egos to life. Help yourself to props.'

Angelique clapped her hands to assemble everyone at the front of the stage. The group dived in, and amongst a chorus of whoops and excited chatter they emerged sporting a selection of wigs, top hats and satin gloves.

Lola shuddered. Playing dress-up really wasn't for her.

'I have the perfect accessory for *you*, Luscious Lola.' Jules approached, sequinned nipple tassels stuck on the outside of her top, and proceeded to hook a shocking pink feather boa around Lola's neck.

'Why, thank you, Juicy Jules.' Lola addressed her friend by her burlesque name, too, and tickled her nose with the end of the fetching neckwear.

As much as she'd prefer to throw on an overcoat and hide from view, she couldn't flat-out refuse to participate and let her friend down. However, the first sign that she was expected to start stripping and she was out of there. It was one thing pratting around with props, but a whole different trauma if it involved taking her clothes off.

Next time Jules suggested a night out Lola would opt for somewhere dark and quiet—like the cinema.

Angelique glided around the dance floor to round up her protégées like glamorous sheep. 'I will show you some basics to get started. First we have the milkshake.'

She shimmied her ample cleavage and encouraged them to do the same.

'I don't have much to shake,' Lola grumbled looking down at her chest. This was *so* not helping her overcome her body issues. Although she didn't look like a flat-chested ten-year-old boy any more, she definitely couldn't pull off *that* move.

'Flaunt what God gave you.' Angelique lifted Lola's arms and shook it for her.

Lola smiled painfully on the outside even as her innards shrivelled up and died of shame. This was her worst nightmare come true. Quite possibly even beating the one about turning up to work naked. At least in that one no one expected her to *pay* for being publicly disgraced. She closed her eyes and prayed for it to stop.

'Good.' The Frenchwoman let her go with a wink. 'Now, we need to get that booty popping, too. Jiggle that *derrière*!'

Lola swore revenge on Jules for making her twerk outside the sanctity of her own home. She gritted her teeth and pretended that shaking her ass was a way she *liked* to pass the time, in case the tactile tutor felt the need to touch her again.

The only thing that stopped her from walking out was the fact that this was an all-female ensemble and not in the least sexually threatening. These women were here for a laugh, and at some point she might actually see the humour, too. Probably when she was at home, safely hidden from grabby French hands.

Interspersed between the tapping of stilettos as the group practised their steps, the scrape of chairs sounded across the wooden floor to put Lola's teeth even more on edge.

'Now take a seat,' Angelique invited them, and tutted when they did. 'Not like that. Like *this*.'

She slid a chair through her legs, seat first, in one fluid movement, and sat astride it.

'With our backsides flush against the back of the chair, we want to pop our legs over the top and lie back, grabbing on to the chair legs. It's all about balance.'

Lola *knew* she should have worn trousers.

Angelique demonstrated a variety of provocative grinding moves until she had her followers riding the furniture like dirty cowgirls. Once Lola's initial discomfort had passed, and she saw that the others were too preoccupied to watch what she was doing, she started to relax into it. This was supposed to be fun—a way to free herself from the tensions of the day, not add to them.

She emptied her mind from all negative thoughts and concentrated on being a good student. After all, this was only a chair, and she was fully dressed. If she stood any chance of moving on from the past she had to stop sweating the small stuff.

Surprisingly, once she let go she found herself enjoying the predatory nature of chair-dancing and the aggressive power it gave her—over the object, over her body. For once she had nothing to prove to anyone, and without the pressure she revelled in her sensuality.

In total abandon, she threw her head back and gave herself over to it—only to lock on to a familiar pair of male chocolate-caramel eyes staring down at her.

'Well, hello, down there…' The masculine French accent mocked her.

From her upside down view it seemed a long way up to find the voice. A pair of muscular jean-clad thighs filled her direct line of sight, but as she glanced up along the slim-fitting blue checked shirt emphasising a solid torso, she met the last face on earth she'd wanted to see smirking back at her.

'Dr Benoit.' Surprise at seeing the head of her department coupled with her awkward position in the chair turned Lola's voice into a husky rasp. Clearly there was a two-for-one deal on nightmares coming true that she hadn't been aware of.

'Dr Roberts.' He gave a slight nod of his head, that lopsided grin never leaving him.

Shame flushed through Lola's system, bringing tension to every muscle as she withdrew into herself. With as much dignity as was available to her in the circumstances, she unhooked her legs and swivelled around to sit in a more civilised pose.

Without the cover of her fellow juniors she had an unimpeded view of her uninvited guest's handsome looks.

There was no denying that the strong smooth jaw and the slightly too-long black hair curling around his ears, along with that accent, gave him all the ingredients for the ultimate heartthrob. But not for her. In her experience good looks tended to hide cruel hearts, and thus far he'd proved no exception.

This little performance simply provided him with more ammo against her. As if it was needed.

'So this is how you spend your time off?' he asked.

Lola got the impression that he thought she would be better employed brushing up on her medical know-how.

The injustice of being caught out on her one night of respite and the sticky heat of embarrassment at her compromising situation crept along her body and made her snap. 'It is no one's business but mine what I do outside hospital hours. So if you'll excuse me…?'

She thought her heart would pound out of her chest as she retaliated. Normally she wouldn't dream of speaking to her superior in such a fashion, but she felt trapped, vulnerable beneath his stare, and she'd learned to fight back whenever she was placed in that situation. She pulled off the suffocating feather boa and made to get up from her chair.

Angelique appeared at her side and placed a restraining hand on her shoulder. 'Stay where you are. Henri's just leaving—aren't you, dear?'

She batted her false lashes and shooed him away—much to Lola's relief.

Henri slunk to the back of the room to take a seat, shaking his head in bewilderment. The familiar scene that had met him behind the studio doors—cackling females sticking their asses out—usually didn't impress him at all. But tonight, seeing one of his staff in Ange's ragtag bunch, had caught him totally off guard.

Lola—that was her name. It really didn't suit her. 'Lola' conjured up images of a showgirl, confident and sure of her every move. The opposite of what she'd shown today. As her supervisor, it now fell to him to draw those qualities from her. One more responsibility to add to his load, and certainly one he could do without.

She obviously had the book smarts to have got this far in her career, but as first appearances went…he was not impressed. He didn't tolerate slacking in his department. Not when he'd already stood by and watched his sister let her medical career slip away without a fight.

Even now Lola appeared to have separated herself from the rest of the group, hiding away in the corner. Although the assertive nature he'd witnessed when he'd walked in and her feisty tone when she'd put him in his place was a complete departure from the hesitant junior doctor he'd encountered earlier.

Relegated to the role of peeping Tom, watching her from the shadows, he was mesmerised by her body-rolls. Every move of her hips showed off the lace-topped stockings under that minuscule skirt and called to his basest needs. Clearly it had been too long since his last hook-up with the opposite sex if the sultry fashion in which Lola straddled the chair seat was making him envy the damn thing!

It wasn't a good idea to be thinking about his new recruit with her bouncy little blonde ponytail and ridiculous pink stethoscope this way. She'd already distracted him from the small matter of his niece's apparent truancy, which he'd come to discuss with Angelique.

Ange stalked over to his corner to wag a finger at him. 'I can't afford to have you scaring off my customers, Henri.'

His older sister gave him that withering look guaranteed to make him regress back into the role of reprimanded teenager. Given the years he'd spent under her wing, he'd had many a rap on the knuckles from her—but he still respected her, and would never purposely do anything to make her regret the sacrifices she had made for him.

'I only said hello,' he muttered, still unable to take his eyes off the performance behind her.

'Well, you shouldn't be in here anyway,' she huffed.

Angelique saved him the trouble of leaving by turning her back on him and ending the session with a round of applause for her trainee dancers.

'*Très bien*. Great stuff, guys. I'm afraid that's all we have time for tonight. I hope you've had fun.'

The flushed, smiling faces staring back at her said it all. Never one to miss an opportunity, she left him to go and hand out her business cards.

'I know this lesson was probably intended as a one-off, but if you want to join us I run classes most evenings. It's a great way to stay in shape and keep the man in your life *very* happy.'

The girls tittered. Henri groaned. He still couldn't quite come to terms with her line of work. Especially when it was his fault she'd traded in a proper career to earn money dancing half naked. If their parents hadn't been killed in that car crash, if Angelique hadn't had to raise a teenage boy on her own, she might have been a respected medical professional by now.

All her studying had gone to waste, her bright future gone in a puff of smoke, in order for her to put food on the table for her little brother. They'd both been handed a life sentence that cold winter's day which had robbed them of their mother and father. And where Angelique seemed to have made peace with the outcome, Henri knew *he* never would. He'd only managed to follow his dreams at the price of his sister's.

The one consolation was that Ange's audience these days mainly consisted of fun-loving females who wanted to learn burlesque, rather than inebriated leering men.

If it hadn't been for one of those men in particular, neither Henri nor Angelique would ever have left Paris for the rain-soaked streets of Northern Ireland. Then again, without the beau who'd enticed his sister to Belfast they wouldn't have Gabrielle and Bastien in their lives—and that was unthinkable, even on the most trying of days.

Henri was forced to wait until Angelique's students had heaped their praises and thanks upon her before he could get a word in.

His patience was wearing thin. They had much more important things to be doing—like trying to figure out why Gabrielle had decided to start skipping school. With Angelique's ex-husband out of the picture, Henri felt even more obligated to his sibling. So much so that he'd undertaken a lot of parental responsibility for the children whose father had long since abandoned them. They needed to get to the bottom of Gabrielle's recent behaviour, but it wasn't a conversation he wished to have with an audience.

'Can we go now? I'm not comfortable as the only eligible male in the company of so many desperate women.'

Angelique turned to him, and only then did Henri realise she wasn't alone. The highlight of his evening stood open-mouthed behind her, emerald eyes now glittering with contempt.

Hands on hips, Lola took a step forward. 'Funny—I didn't get the memo that said we "desperate women" were dancing for anyone else's benefit other than our own.'

Henri cursed himself for the overheard harsh words that had caused Lola's soft pink lips to draw into a tight line.

Her features only softened when she addressed her instructor again. 'Thanks for an enjoyable night and it was lovely to meet you.'

Lola tossed her golden mane of hair over her shoulder

and, with self-righteous grace, made her exit, Henri put firmly in his place. The woman definitely had bite, and that had succeeded in piquing his interest. If only he could get her to show that passion and spirit in the workplace…

'*Idiot!*'

Ange brought him back into the room. With half their lives having been spent living and working in Northern Ireland their native tongue had almost been rendered a distant memory, but her accent increased when she was angry—and, boy, was she angry.

'I'm sorry. I didn't mean anything by it. I was just—'

'I know you don't like what I do, Henri, but this is how I make my living and you can't be rude to my customers. Maybe it's better if you stay away from now on.'

Ange didn't give him a chance to explain his irritability as she threw props back into the box with a ferocity Henri knew she wanted to direct at him.

'I won't say another word. Promise. I'll help you get locked up and then I'll take you home.'

Where they could both confront his niece about what was going on. The only reason he hadn't said anything to Gabrielle himself since the phone call from her headmistress was because he didn't want to step on Angelique's toes. It was *her* daughter they were dealing with, after all.

'Thanks, but I'll walk.' She pulled on a mac over her scant outfit and flicked off the lights.

'You can't go out there like that!'

Henri forgot himself and once again voiced his concern about her fashion sense, regardless that she'd reminded him time and time again that he wasn't her father. He couldn't help himself. It didn't bear thinking about that something should happen to the only important woman in his life and he hadn't attempted to prevent it.

'I'm an adult, Henri. I can look after myself, and sooner or later you're going to have to realise that.'

She all but shoved him out through the door, and Henri was given the brush-off by a second woman in as many minutes.

Lola kept her back ramrod-straight until she reached her car and crumpled into the front seat. She had taken the opportunity to have a private word with Angelique when Jules and the others had gone on to the pub, toying with the idea of continuing the lessons in an effort to kick-start her self-esteem.

Textbooks were great for swotting up, but they didn't help her deal with people face-to-face—and, for her, that remained the most daunting element of her job. For every model citizen she encountered, there were going to be times when she was alone with aggressive patients, or cocky men who couldn't keep their hands to themselves. She knew that, and accepted it, but she also knew she needed to get into the right frame of mind to deal with it effectively.

The protocol for those situations probably *wasn't* to burst into tears and curl into a ball. It would take even more bravery than she'd mustered to leave home and go through medical school, to tell potential troublemakers to back off with any authority.

Until this evening she hadn't realised how much inner strength she possessed. Dancing had helped her explore a side of herself she hadn't known existed, and she would embrace all the help available to embark on this new phase of her life and overcome her fears. It was too bad that Mr Ego of the Year had taken that sliver of newfound confidence and crushed it underfoot.

Lola groaned, predicting that the repercussions of to-night's ill-tempered exchange would surely be felt at work.

She couldn't remember the last time she'd spoken to anyone like that—never mind a man with the power to make or break her career. But the fault totally lay at Henri Benoit's feet. He had no business crossing paths with her outside the hospital and insulting her when she'd been so exposed. For an unguarded moment she'd let light break through the darkness, only for him to cast her back in shadow. The problem was she had no way of explaining that—or her defensive reaction to it—if he decided to haul her over the coals tomorrow.

'I won't cry,' she said out loud, determined not to let another arrogant male reduce her to a gibbering wreck.

Engine started, she threw her Mini into Reverse and put her foot on the accelerator.

A loud bang and the jolt of the car caused her to slam on the brakes.

She didn't dare look.

Whatever she'd hit, she couldn't afford it.

Outside, she heard a car door open and close, heavy footsteps coming towards her. She switched off the ignition and braced herself, but the footsteps had stopped—no doubt to survey the damage.

'Mon Dieu!'

The foreign curse instantly gave away the identity of her victim.

Lola closed her eyes. *Oh, please. Not him!*

She slowly unclipped her seat belt and got out of the car to enter into the fearful realm of the Frenchman's ire.

'I'm sorry,' she said, knowing she didn't sound a fraction apologetic.

He bent down to inspect the cracked registration plate of his red sports car. *Typical.* She couldn't have hit a clapped-out rust heap—it would *have* to be this shiny status symbol.

'Is this payback for what I said in there?'

The patronising tone he used grated on Lola's already sensitive last nerve.

'I'm not that petty. Besides, it's only the number plate that looks damaged.' It wasn't as though she'd written off his boy toy altogether.

'Does your clown car not come with mirrors fitted?'

He looked down his high-bridged nose at her with a smug expression she wanted to slap off his face. The car she drove was a luxury, allowed her by the generosity of her brothers, who'd painstakingly restored it from its rusty former self and made it hers with a bubblegum-pink respray. Not everyone was afforded the life of privilege she imagined he'd led, and any snooty slight against her family was the one thing guaranteed to make her blood boil.

'I would have thought your ego was big enough to use as a force field and deflect the Pink Peril.'

With three elder brothers, exchanging childish insults came as naturally as breathing for Lola. She already had a black mark against her for squaring up to him, so she might as well make it count. Besides, *he'd* gone down the snarky route first.

'The *Pink Peril*?' he echoed incredulously and the grin grew into a full-on beaming smile.

He was treading on dangerous ground now.

'My brothers named it,' she huffed, and told her easily pleased inner schoolgirl, which was squealing with hormonal appreciation at the appearance of man dimples, to shut up. It was surely another sign of trauma manifesting itself that she found a man insulting her attractive.

'Do I take it that's a reference to your driving skills?' His eyes shone with suppressed laughter, the skin creasing at the corners to elevate his hunk status.

'I have *excellent* driving skills,' she protested.

'So I see.' He lifted a thick dark brow as he glanced back at the damage.

'Look, I've apologised. I'll pay for repairs. So, if we're done here…?'

It was time she left—before she completely shot down her career. This man seemingly brought out the worst in her, and that wasn't conducive to a happy six weeks under his tutelage.

Far from helping her get over the day's trials and tribulations, this whole evening had simply heaped more stress upon her. At least with this latest disaster she knew she could count on her brothers to make any necessary repairs with the minimum of fuss. If only they could come to work with her tomorrow and clear up the mess she'd made there, too, she might have a chance of clawing back some respect.

'I think I have an apology of my own to make. I didn't mean to insult you in there.'

Henri ignored her need to end the conversation and perched his butt on the bonnet of his precious car.

'And yet you did.' She folded her arms across her chest as he brought up the subject of his slur against her character once more. He couldn't know the throwaway insult had hit her on such a personal level, but that didn't give him the right to end up the good guy here.

'The problem is between Angelique and myself. I shouldn't have taken it out on you. It's fair to say I don't exactly approve of the work she does.' A shake of his head emphasised his dismay.

'She seems like a woman who knows her own mind.' Lola didn't imagine a free spirit such as Angelique needed his permission to do something she obviously loved.

'Ah, but Ange doesn't always know what's *best* for her.'

The sincerity Henri expressed brought goosebumps along Lola's skin. Even though he might not agree with his other half's lifestyle choice, his devotion was beyond doubt. The only unconditional love Lola had ever had was from her brothers. The tragic tale of her failed past relationships was entirely to do with her reluctance to let anyone else get close. She considered Angelique a very lucky woman.

'It's chilly out here, so if we could get back to rectifying this mess I would like to get home. I really think your licence plate took the full impact, and I can get my brother to order you a new one. I hardly think it warrants involving insurance companies.'

What went on behind the doors of *chez* Benoit was none of her business—she certainly didn't want to warm towards the man responsible for ruining her entire day. All she wanted to do now was call it quits and start afresh tomorrow.

'In that case we can sort the details out at work. I can see you're in a hurry.'

He finally took the hint and Lola dashed back to her car to wait for him to move.

As she sat with her arms locked out straight, holding on to the steering wheel for dear life, she exhaled slowly. Everything seemed to hit her at once, and her heart started drumming so hard she thought she might just pass out.

One night of escapism, thinking she could be 'normal', and she'd played stripper, crashed her car and had another run-in with her boss—embarrassing herself at every step. It was more excitement in her life than she cared for.

The next six weeks working under Henri Benoit stretched before her like a prison sentence. One with absolutely no chance of getting time off for good behaviour.

CHAPTER TWO

BUILT TO SERVE the influx of inhabitants to the rejuvenated city, the predominantly glass and marble structure of the Belfast Community Hospital was bright and modern. Even now she was in the bustling corridors, under the glare of fluorescent light, Lola thought it a beautiful building.

These last few shifts had shown her that any chance for silent contemplation ended on the far side of the double doors, and Lola braced herself for the madness of A&E on a Friday night as she pushed them open.

'Nurse! Nurse!'

The loud, slurred speech of a waiting patient greeted her. A hand shot out and clamped around her wrist, immediately regressing her to that time in her life when she hadn't had the strength to fight back.

She screwed her eyes tightly shut, in an attempt to fend off the memories assaulting her, but it only succeeded in leaving her alone in the dark with them.

The busy reception area faded away, and the walls closed in until she was back in that small room crammed full of grinning faces. Her limbs were immobile, pinned down by unseen forces, leaving her completely at the mercy of her attackers. They were too strong for her, their hands tugging at her clothes until she was naked and shivering beneath them.

The actual assault had lasted only minutes—long enough to satisfy their cruel need to break her spirit. Once her humiliation was complete, the matter of her sexuality no longer an issue, they'd thrown her clothes at her and walked away. In hindsight, her ordeal could have been much worse, even though it hadn't felt like that at the time.

A shudder racked through Lola's body as she contemplated the alternative. It had taken her years even to let another man touch her after that betrayal, and she doubted she would ever have recovered if that band of delinquents had decided to take things any further.

The intervening years had been tough for her as she'd tried to come to terms with what her bullies had probably deemed no more than a prank. For her, the experience had left her wanting to run from the room screaming if a man so much as put his hands on her uninvited. Only her desire to practice medicine on the general public had put her on the road to recovery and stopped her freaking out completely at times like this.

The pressure eased from around her forearm, immediately releasing her from her torment. She blinked her eyes open to see a man she guessed to be in his sixties slumped in a plastic chair beside her. After a deep breath she extricated his fingers from her person and reminded herself that she wasn't a helpless teen any more.

'I'm Dr Roberts. I'm sure one of the nurses will be along shortly to assess your condition, sir.'

He had a small gash on his right cheek, which was letting a small trickle of blood further colour his already ruddy features, but she suspected from the stench of alcohol closing in around her that alcohol was the main reason behind his hospital visit.

'Am I dying, Doctor?' Red-rimmed eyes tried to focus on her, and it soon became obvious he was more of a danger to himself than anyone else.

It buoyed her confidence to know she was the one in control of the situation here, and she was able to reassure him with a pat on the hand. 'I'm pretty sure you're not dying, but I'll send someone over to see you as soon as possible.'

'Good.' He sank back into the chair, placated for now, and the sound of tuneless singing followed her on her way.

With the patient's concerns passed on to one of the nurses, with the advice that it might be wise to have him seen to and discharged before he settled down for the night, Lola lifted a file from the stack on the desk.

Her first patient was an elderly woman experiencing dizziness and fatigue. Possible dehydration, since the notes indicated an increased thirst and decreased skin turgor. No doubt this lady had been specifically left for Lola to deal with because of the apparently straightforward nature of the ailment, but she didn't mind. The role of general dogsbody gave her inner wallflower a chance to disappear under paperwork and the smaller jobs more experienced doctors deemed too trivial to waste their talents on. These small steps into the medical field would carry her through until it was her moment to shine. At which point she might need some anti-anxiety pills to hand.

With her bits and pieces gathered together from the storeroom, she made her way to the cubicle. The sight of the elderly lady waiting for her behind the curtain immediately put her at ease.

'Now, then, Mrs Jackson. I'm just going to take a wee blood sample from you, if that's all right?' A UE blood test would tell if the electrolytes and sodium were off—a further indication of dehydration.

The old woman smiled, the skin at the corners of her pale blue eyes creasing with laughter. 'Sure, I'm like a pin cushion these days anyway.'

Lola noted how sunken her eyes looked, and the dryness of her lips when she smiled. The dry mucus membranes were another sure sign her diagnosis was correct.

'So I don't need to worry about you passing out when you see this needle?' If only all her patients were this co-operative it would make her job a whole lot easier.

'No, dear. You do what you have to.' Like a professional blood donor, Mrs Jackson held out her arm and tapped on a raised blue vein. 'That's where they usually go for.'

The translucent skin was already punctuated with fading bruises from similar procedures. Lola cleansed the area with a wipe, grateful that she wouldn't have to put this lovely lady through the ordeal of chasing a suitable site to insert the needle.

'I think you could get yourself a job here,' Lola said as she tightened the tourniquet around the upper arm.

'Ach, away with you. I could never put in the hours you youngsters do. Sure, when would you ever find time to catch yourself a husband? Unless you're waiting for one of those handsome male doctors to sweep you off your feet?'

The inquisitive patient brought an uninvited picture of the suave Henri Benoit into Lola's head. Even there he looked smug that she was thinking about him.

'If you could just make a fist for me that would be great. Now, you'll feel a little scratch,' Lola said as she inserted the needle and let the woman's last question fall without an answer.

Thankfully she had managed to avoid said handsome doctor and the embarrassment of that evening thus far. So why did her senses conspire and refuse to let her forget him? The sound of his accent, the smell of his aftershave and the memory of his rarely seen smile wouldn't leave her. It was a godsend that their hands had only touched briefly or she would surely have ended up a victim of sensory overload.

She tried desperately hard not to think about taste.

Since that final humiliation at the club, he was the last person she would turn to for help. She wouldn't give him the satisfaction of seeing her inadequacy in action. Regardless of how many times she carried out standard procedures confidently and correctly, she couldn't shake off that look of disappointment he'd given her. Her fender bender in the car park had been the only time she'd witnessed the scowl slip from the registrar's face and the smile had somehow been worse. It had made him human, showed a softer side to him, and it had made her want to impress him so she could see it again.

'Could you hold that cotton wool for me there, Mrs Jackson?' Lola withdrew the needle and the helpful patient dabbed the spot of blood left behind. 'Now, you rest until we find a bed for you on the ward, and I'll get these sent off.'

'Thank you, dear.' The previously animated pensioner lay back, flattening her head of white curls into the pillows, and showed the first signs of fatigue.

Lola vowed to take all the necessary steps to get Mrs Jackson rehydrated and back on her feet as she returned to the nurses' station—and walked into a flurry of activity.

'What's going on?' she asked Jules, who was passing by in the herd of medics apparently gearing up for something more serious than an old dear having a turn.

'Emergency call. Ambulance is on the way with a patient in cardiac arrest.'

As Jules chewed on her pen Lola could see her body thrumming with anticipation for the arrival. Maybe it was the extra year's experience Jules had over her, but Lola hadn't quite reached that stage of life-or-death excitement.

'Would you care to join us, Dr Roberts?'

Apparently it took the invitation to be issued in a French accent to get her pulse racing.

'Pardon?' She turned to face Dr Benoit, incredulous

that he had asked her to participate as if he was issuing
an invitation to dinner.

'I'm sure they can spare you from treating minor cases
for a while, and I think the experience will be good for
you.'

He barely glanced in her direction and carried on flicking through his notes. A prod of disappointment poked
Lola in the abdomen as he dropped back into aloof doctor mode. A far cry from her sparring partner in the car
park, but at least she knew where she stood with this version of Henri Benoit—and she wouldn't let him get the
better of her.

Lola lifted her chin to meet the challenge. 'I would love
to join the team.'

Equipment gathered in preparation, the assembled medical staff waited for the starting pistol, ready to get off the
blocks, whilst Lola willed her limbs to stop shaking. The
paramedics slammed through the door and galvanised everyone else into action.

Here we go.

'On the count of three.' Henri took charge as they surrounded the trolley. 'One, two, three.'

Between the paramedics and the doctors the seemingly
lifeless body of an overweight middle-aged man was trans-
ferred from the stretcher onto the bed and hooked up to a
bank of monitors.

'Get a line in, please, Lola,' Henri instructed.

With a very small chance of bringing the patient back,
there was no room for her to freeze or panic.

'Starting CPR,' Henri announced, starting chest com-
pressions.

Lola's scrubs clung to her suddenly clammy skin as
she fought to insert the cannula. They needed it to inject
adrenaline and try to restart the heart, and he had tasked

her with the important job. Thankfully, with Henri pumping the chest to get blood and oxygen flowing around the body again, he made it possible for her to find a vein.

'I'm in.' She managed to keep the relief from her voice in a room full of people who did this every day of the week.

'Get the paddles on. Do we have a shockable rhythm?'

Henri's voice carried above all other noise and she focused on it alone to guide her through what was happening.

'Everyone stand back. Shock delivered. One milligram of adrenaline in. Stop for rhythm, please.'

They paused and listened for signs of life. Nothing. More chest pumps, more adrenaline and more shocks were delivered by the defibrillator to kick-start the heart—until he uttered the words she longed to hear.

'He's back.'

Lola stood back in awe as Henri's cool command brought a dead man back to life, indicated by the steady blip of his pulse on the screen.

Once the patient was stabilised Henri addressed the team. 'Good job, everyone. Lola, you too. You can go back to what you were doing.'

That commanding tone had turned softer, something she was unaccustomed to, and it was a wonder she heard it above the pounding of blood in her ear as the last minutes caught up with her.

Unable to speak, she flashed him a grateful smile and made her way out of the resuscitation room. The less frantic corridor outside was a welcome respite from the drama, and Lola took a minute to catch her breath. Only now did the reality hit her that she had played a part in saving a man's life. With no time to worry over who was watching as she administered the adrenaline, she had acted on pure instinct and skill.

A hand rested on her shoulder and forced Lola to concentrate on not collapsing onto the polished floor.

'Are you okay?'

Henri's brown eyes bored into hers until she felt her feet gradually slipping from under her.

He directed her to a seat. 'Here, sit down.'

'I'm fine. Really,' she insisted, wanting him to disappear as quickly as he'd arrived and leave her to stew in her own embarrassment.

'It is okay to have a little wobble.'

His pronunciation of that last word sounded so ridiculous for the sophisticated doctor she felt better already.

'These things—they are intense and difficult to handle at the beginning, but you did your job. You were part of the team that brought him back and you should be proud of yourself, Lola. Now, take five minutes and get yourself a cup of tea whilst it's quiet.'

As he left her Lola couldn't be sure if it was the first sign of compassion from him or his continued use of her first name that had sent another bolt of adrenaline to bring her own body back to life.

On doctor's orders she soon found herself in the canteen, paying for a cure-all cuppa. Her first time as part of the resus team had left her a little shaky on her feet, so she couldn't wait to sit down and take a time-out.

A 'Bonjour!' much too cheery for it to have come from her superior greeted her in the seating area. The familiar figure of her burlesque instructor waved her over to a table in the corner.

'Come and join us. I didn't know you worked here. I take it you and Henri know each other?'

Angelique, dressed more conservatively than the last time Lola had seen her, directed her to a seat. She was accompanied by a teenage girl who bore an uncanny resemblance to Henri and his other half. It was unfair that one family had hogged all the would-look-good-in-a-bin-bag genes.

Naturally any child with that combination of DNA in her genetic make-up was bound to be a beauty, but she'd clearly been in the wars. Her otherwise clear skin was marred by a series of angry red abrasions across her cheek, whilst the beginnings of a purple bruise ringed her right eye.

'You could say that. I've just started my placement in A&E. I'm Lola, by the way.' She introduced herself to the Benoit mini-me as she sat down with her tea.

'Gabrielle,' the girl mumbled, in that barely comprehensible manner all teenagers used in the presence of strangers.

'Are you here to see Henri?'

'Yes, but they told us he's busy with a patient. We'll just have to wait until he comes home to speak to him.' Angelique shifted restlessly in her seat, clearly more bothered about not seeing him than she was willing to let on.

'We were dealing with an emergency admission downstairs, but I'm sure he'll be free soon. Is there anything I can help you with in the meantime? If you want I can take you down after this and take a look at those cuts on your face?'

Lola turned her attention to the young girl, with her head bowed as she played with the food on her plate, a curtain of raven hair now falling over her face to hide the marks from view.

'That won't be necessary, thanks. The school nurse cleaned Gabrielle up before they phoned me to collect her. It's nothing serious, but they don't take any chances these days.'

Angelique's fidgety hands on the table gave away her real concern, and Lola thought perhaps she was simply being polite and didn't want to bother her.

'It's no trouble. As you say, it's better to be safe than sorry.' Besides, she was sure Henri wouldn't take too kindly to finding out his daughter had been sent away without some sort of examination.

'I'm fine. I tripped and fell in the playground—it's not a big deal.' The surly teen rested back on her chair, arms folded across her chest, practically daring Lola to disagree.

'Honestly, that's not even why we're here. We have a cake emergency that requires immediate attention. So, unless you know someone who can whip up a dinosaur-themed birthday cake in twenty-four hours, I'm afraid you can't help.'

A diplomatic Angelique stepped in to change the subject to one even closer to Lola's heart than her job.

'Whose birthday is it?'

'My son's. Bastien will be six tomorrow, and he's decided at the last minute that the only thing he wants is a dinosaur cake. I can't find one in the supermarkets, and bakeries need more notice than I can give. I was hoping to brainstorm with Henri—or get him to take a crash course in baking.'

The stressed mother let out a sigh as she planted an image in Lola's brain of the usually suave doctor up to his elbows in flour.

'I've been known to do a bit of baking myself.'

That was like saying Beyoncé did a bit of singing. The kitchen was Lola's natural habitat, and where she went to unwind at the end of the day. She didn't usually do commissions, but she'd made all manner of themed cakes for her brothers over the years. Where money had been scarce, imagination had been plentiful. A dinosaur might be fun.

'Are you saying you could do it?' This time Gabrielle appeared to be totally enamoured by her new acquaintance, her dark eyes shining with excitement.

Lola understood the love a sister had for a brother, and the need to see him happy even when he could be a royal pain in the butt at times.

'Maybe…I mean, I'm no expert or anything…' She knew she was capable of doing it, but those doubts crept in that her standards mightn't be good enough for a third party.

'I don't care if it's nothing more than a blob with eyes and scales, as long as I have something to give him. You're a lifesaver. Now, if you could have it ready by tonight, I can send Henri to get it. How much do you need for supplies, et cetera?'

Angelique began to rifle in her handbag, immediately dampening Lola's spirit. She baked out of love—not for financial gain.

'Whoa! I haven't agreed to do it yet. What if Henri doesn't want me involved? He sees enough of me here.'

There was also the matter of Lola not being thrilled with the idea of crossing paths with him again outside of work. She'd only just sorted out the last mess she'd made—with Jake's help. He'd stepped in and dealt with the aftermath of the fender bender so she didn't have to.

'It's not Henri's call.'

Lola didn't want to end up in the middle of a domestic dispute, especially when she really didn't know these people.

She drained her cup and stood to leave, hoping they would follow suit. 'Why don't we check with him anyway, before we make any definite plans?'

Henri probably wouldn't deny the child his birthday wish, but Lola couldn't afford to stuff things up again. As far as she was concerned this was *his* call.

Henri might have broken his vow to keep his distance from the pink princess after his lapse at the club, but it was worth it if his interference today had boosted her confidence even a fraction.

He knew Lola's capabilities were there, if she could just

stop overthinking her every move. Whilst her job meant being able to assess a situation, it also meant being decisive. Aside from her fine display of booty-shaking, today was the first time he had seen her act without second-guessing herself. If a push out of her comfort zone was what it took to make a doctor out of her, then as her superior he felt obliged to continue. It was absolutely nothing to do with him getting a kick out of seeing her fired up.

Once Henri had made sure his coronary patient was stable he went to his office to strip off his scrub top. He could shower at home, but for now a clean shirt would help peel away the layers of stress from the day.

I know there's one in here somewhere.

He pulled open drawer after drawer, until a light tap on the office door interrupted his shirt search.

'Come in.'

'Dr Benoit…' Lola's voice trailed off as she caught him half-naked. Her wide eyes registered his state of undress, then shot towards the floor, the ceiling—anywhere but his bare chest.

'What is it?' he snapped, miffed by her visual dismissal. A white T-shirt rolled up at the back of his bottom drawer saved him from self-doubt and he pulled it on over his head.

'Angelique and Gabrielle are here. I…er…thought you would want to know.'

She scuttled away but Henri caught up and grabbed her arm.

'Where are they? Is something wrong?'

Lola let out a yelp and wrestled out of his grasp. 'They're outside. Gabrielle has taken a tumble at school, but insists she's fine, and Angelique wants to talk to you about Bastien's birthday. I'm just making sure you aren't too busy to see them.'

Lola backed away, rubbing the skin on her arm where he'd grabbed her.

Henri immediately regretted being so rough. He hadn't meant to scare her, but the thought of the girls in trouble had made him act without thinking.

'I always have time for my family.'

'In that case I'll show them in.' Lola frowned at him, making no attempt to hide her displeasure at his behaviour, and rightly so.

'Thank you, and…er…sorry about—' He gestured towards her arm when he realised *Sorry for manhandling you* would sound totally inappropriate.

'It's okay.' She managed a half smile before she opened the door to let Angelique in.

Gabrielle followed her mother inside and Henri spotted the red marks crisscrossing her pale skin. Emotion overwhelmed him once again. 'What the hell happened?'

'It's just superficial,' the rational voice of his junior assured him, even though he could see that for himself.

It didn't stop him from worrying.

'Gabrielle? How did this happen to you?'

His niece gave an exaggerated *tut*. 'I keep telling everyone it's no big deal. I fell over. End of story.'

Henri knew he wasn't getting the whole picture when she turned her face towards the wall and refused to look at him.

Out of the corner of his eye he could see Angelique's shake of the head, meant only for him—an indication that he wasn't to pursue the matter any further. It wasn't in his nature to stand idly by and pretend things was okay when they blatantly weren't, but in parental matters he had to defer to his sister.

'At least get a cold compress for that eye to stop the swelling.'

'I'll do it when I get home.' An eye roll accompanied the insinuation that he was being a fusspot.

'I actually wanted to talk to you about Bastien's birthday. He's changed his mind about a pirate party and decided he wants a dinosaur cake instead.'

The uncle/niece stand-off ended with Angelique's intervention and a completely different tangent in the conversation.

Now Henri was the one rolling his eyes. His young nephew changed his mind more often than Angelique changed costumes. The never-ending parade of after-school activities as he bored easily with one and moved on to the next attested to that. There wasn't time for a dull moment with him around, and Henri's life was the better for it. Without his sister and the kids to occupy his thoughts he'd probably be just another self-absorbed playboy, like so many he'd met in the profession.

'Surely that's an easy fix and not one that warrants Dr Roberts's time?' Lord knew what Lola must think, being called away from her patients to deal with trivial family matters. Especially when he'd called her out on her first day of placement for doing exactly the same thing.

'Not as straightforward as you might think at such short notice, and Lola has offered to help out. She thought we should get *your* approval before moonlighting as our personal cake decorator.'

There was definitely more than a hint of sarcasm there as his big sister was forced to change the dynamics of their relationship by asking his permission to do anything. Lola stood quietly waiting for his approval and he got the impression she'd been strong-armed into helping.

'You dance *and* bake?'

He was learning something new about her every day. Probably more than he should. Events seemed to be conspiring against him—and his rule about not fraternising with his A&E colleagues outside of work. He had doctor friends, of course, but he preferred not to muddy the waters between himself and the junior staff.

Apart from friendships becoming strained when he had to exert his authority at work, there was also the temporary nature of their position here. There was little point in forging new relationships which detracted from his family responsibilities only for them to move on to their next placement. Not that he was anticipating spending any more time with Lola than was normal—she just seemed to *be* there, everywhere he turned.

'I do one much better than the other.'

The woman in question flushed pink as she underplayed her talents, but Henri had seen her in action.

'Well, I *know* you can dance…' He watched the bloom rise in her cheeks at the reminder that he'd seen her moves in all their glory.

Until that moment when he'd witnessed Lola giving herself over to the music he'd never seen the beauty of burlesque. Thus far it had represented everything he hated about life after his parents' deaths—the financial struggle and the guilt he harboured for being Angelique's responsibility when she was nothing more than a kid herself. That perception had altered when he'd watched burlesque empower a shy doctor before his eyes. It had brought Henri some understanding of his sister's insistence that she danced for no one but herself.

If it hadn't been for Angelique coughing, Henri might have forgotten he and Lola weren't alone in the room.

'So, Lola can make the cake and you will pick it up from her house tonight, Henri—yes?'

'Wait…what?'

'Great. You two can sort out the details and Gabrielle and I will go and buy the rest of the party supplies. Thanks again for offering to help out.'

Angelique swallowed Lola into her embrace in that gregarious manner which made it impossible to say no to the woman. The mere mention of culinary skills and Henri's unassuming colleague would have been a lamb to the slaughter in her presence. And even he now found himself roped into paying Lola an out-of-hours visit when it was the last thing he wanted to do.

Still, it wouldn't do to make a scene and have her think there was an issue. It was simply a matter of keeping his nephew happy. He'd have a discreet word with his sister later, about not putting him into compromising positions with his staff in future.

Lola watched open-mouthed as the French tornado blasted back out through the door, taking her offspring with her and leaving a trail of destruction in her wake. Henri was frozen to the spot, probably wondering what the hell he'd agreed to. Somehow Lola's offer to bake a cake had led to an appointment with Henri at her apartment. Her safe haven was about to be breached by the one man who could bring her temper to a boil with one flick of a switch.

Without Angelique's huge personality to fill the room Lola found herself alone with Henri in his tight white T-shirt. Although she was off men for the foreseeable future, it didn't mean she was immune to fine man candy. She could still picture his half-naked body when she'd walked in earlier—the speed bump abs and the trail of dark hair dipping from his navel into the waistband of his trousers, reminding her that he had the body to match the hint of sexy in his eyes.

It was enough to give her the vapours, trying to match the creases in his shirt with the defined muscles she'd only caught a glimpse of.

An awkward silence ticked between them as Lola played a game of hide and seek with his abs. At some point she was either going to have to make conversation or ask him for a quick flash to get reacquainted with his six-pack. She chose the option less likely to start a cat fight with his significant other.

'If you have a pen and paper to hand, I'll write my address down for you.'

'Of course.' Henri, too, snapped back to life and scrabbled on his desk for the requested stationery. 'I'm sorry if you've been inconvenienced. Angelique takes no prisoners, I'm afraid.'

'It's all right. What kind of person would I be to leave the birthday boy without a dinosaur cake? Anyway, I should think this makes us even now. I hit your car—I bake you a cake. Debt repaid.'

After this there was no reason for either of them to venture into each other's social territory, or for her to ogle her registrar again. The image of him stripped to the waist was imprinted on her brain for ever anyway.

She handed him the piece of paper with her hastily scribbled address. 'I'll need a couple of hours after work to get it done. Shall we say eight o'clock?'

Her steady voice belied her insides as they danced a jig at the thought of him waiting on her doorstep. She wasn't particularly relishing explaining it all to Jules, either.

'Eight's fine by me. Whatever it takes to have at least *one* happy child to go home to.'

The way Henri raked his hand through his hair told of his anxiety over one young person in particular.

'Gabrielle?'

He nodded. 'The bruises, the truancy…there's clearly something going on, but she refuses to tell us what.'

Lola knew he had to be confiding in her out of desperation—by all accounts he was usually a private man. She wasn't an authority on the subject of raising children,

but she had been a teenage girl with bruises and excuses
to avoid school.

'I hate to say this, but do you think there could be anything going on at school?'

Henri fixed her with an unwavering stare until she
found it difficult to breathe, fearing she'd overstepped the
mark. After a few heart-stopping seconds he let out a long
sigh and brought her some much needed relief.

'She says not—goes mad at the suggestion I pay her
teachers a visit—but it's getting to the stage where I might
have to.'

Lola could imagine him going in, that feisty French
temper at full blast, making things much worse for the
young girl. Her brothers hadn't improved matters for *her*
when they'd gone storming in with their fists flying.

'I'm sure she'll confide in you when the time's right for
her. It's not easy for teenage girls to talk to anyone—especially their daddy.'

There'd been absolutely no point in Lola going to *her*
daddy at the height of the bullying—he wouldn't have
coped when he'd barely been able to hold himself together.
Lola's relationship with her father now was somehow more
distant than the one with her estranged mother. He was
still around, but he'd never been the parent she'd needed.
If Lola ever had children of her own she hoped they'd have
a man like Henri in their lives to genuinely care for them.

Just as she was getting carried away by the *aww* factor
of Henri looking out for his baby girl, she caught sight of
his raised eyebrow and lopsided smile.

'What? I'm forbidden to voice an opinion? Trust me—
you'll do her no favours by storming in and ignoring her
wishes. Be there for her...let her know she can come to
you when the time is right.'

Her speech had been a long time coming, and it was
one meant for her own family, but it was as relevant to this

situation as it had been then. Henri and Angelique needed to open the lines of communication with their daughter before things got any worse.

The adrenaline rush of speaking out left Lola dizzy and a little breathless.

Henri tilted his head to the side and gave her a grin that sent shivers through her very core. 'You think I'm Gabrielle's *father*?'

She didn't want to say yes and compound her mistake, since he was making it very apparent he wasn't. 'Father, stepfather, whatever… You're still her guardian.'

'I'm her uncle.'

'Oh. *Oh*.' The implications of that new information slowly filtered through to Lola's brain. If she was his niece, that meant—

'Angelique is my sister.'

He put an end to her struggle to put the pieces together and garnered another performance of her goldfish impression.

'I just assumed… You're clearly a very close family.'

She must have been blinded by their combined beauty not to notice the now obvious resemblance between them. Beautiful people always gravitated towards each other, so Lola had never imagined either one of the Benoits as singletons. If they were. For all she knew there could be more Model Trons stashed away—robots disguised as physically perfect humans whose mission on Earth was to make everyone who wasn't a perfect ten seem like a frump in comparison.

'Are you telling me you thought Angelique and I were a *couple*?'

A deep, rumbling laugh reverberated around the room and reduced Lola back to that bumbling rookie who knew nothing.

'I put two and two together—' She shrugged her shoulders as she chalked up another nomination for the Idiot of the Month award.

'And you came up with five. I guess we *are* closer than most since our parents died. When Angelique left Paris to be with the kids' father I decided to come and do my studies here and keep what was left of the family together.'

A sadness settled over Henri, stealing the twinkle from his smile as he spoke of his loss. It explained the close bond he had with his sister and her children. Hadn't Lola clung to her brothers, too, when their parents had bailed?

'And Angelique's partner is no longer on the scene?' It wasn't really any of her business, but if he was in a sharing mood it was better to find out the exact circumstances before she put her foot in it again.

Henri shook his head. 'Sean's been in and out of her life, but I think she's better off without him.'

'At least she has you to help out with the children and broker her cake deals.'

It was Lola's turn to have some fun and lighten the atmosphere before she was expected to reveal personal information in return. Although she no longer saw him as her arch nemesis, neither was he a friend. At least not one whom she was ready to trust with her deepest, darkest secrets.

'There is that.'

Henri's frown evened out into another smile and Lola was able to appreciate the beauty of it guilt-free now she knew he and Angelique weren't romantically involved.

'Well, I guess I'll see you at eight o'clock, then.' Lola cleared her throat and brought an abrupt end to the conversation. Today had been full of revelations, and she saw no need to explore any more. Henri was attractive and single. No big deal.

'I'll be there at eight to pick up the cake. You know—

the one for *my sister*?' He teased her one last time before she left the office.

With the door firmly closed behind her, Lola rested her head against it and tried to regulate her heartbeat. There was bound to be a logical explanation for the flutter of her pulse every time Henri reminded her that he was un-attached, and as a qualified doctor she was determined to find a cure.

CHAPTER THREE

HENRI TOOK THE slip road off the motorway and followed the now familiar route to Lola's apartment block in the Titanic Quarter. Next to Belfast Lough, and just a stone's throw away from where the *Titanic* had cast off her moorings, this area was highly sought after. He'd been surprised, after he'd followed the sat-nav here previously to collect the cake, to find a junior doctor could afford such luxury.

'We're here,' he announced, pulling on the car's handbrake.

Gabrielle remained slumped in the passenger seat next to him, staring out through the rain-splattered window.

'What about my chicken?' a small voice piped up from the back seat.

Henri saw Bastien in the rearview mirror with his arms folded and lips pursed, ready for a full-on tantrum.

'Don't worry. We're just here to thank the lady for making your cake and drop off her dish—then we'll get a bucket of secret chicken as soon as we're finished.'

Their 'secret' chicken had nothing to do with a recipe and everything to do with not telling Angelique. She would kill him if she found out he was filling her children with fast food, but he didn't want to deal with dinnertime dramatics tonight. Not when he was under strict instructions to make amends for not inviting Lola to Bastien's party.

If he hadn't spent most of the day before the party wrapped up in department meetings he might have saved himself the trouble of a house call now, but he hadn't seen her since taking delivery of the fabulous cake-osaurus.

'Can we get ice-cream, too?' The six-year-old bounced in and out of view.

'We'll see.'

Henri didn't give a definitive answer, but these kids knew how to wrap their uncle round their little fingers. If only Gabrielle would show similar signs of enthusiasm. She was quiet and withdrawn, and it scared the hell out of him.

Angelique had tried talking to her before work, but other than another 'I'm fine', there had been no progress. Henri hated watching his niece's pain from the sidelines when it was his job to help others, his duty to care for his family. But all he could do for now was heed Lola's advice and stay by her side.

Gabrielle unclipped her seat belt and exited the car without the usual coaxing it took to get her out in public. The eager exit boded well. Perhaps Lola's company would be enough to put a smile on her face.

Henri knew he should have phoned ahead when Lola answered the door wearing a pig-patterned fleecy all-in-one.

'Dr Benoit!' Her cheeks turned the same shade of cute pink as her nightwear. 'I...er...wasn't expecting visitors tonight.' She dropped her eyes to her matching pig-shaped slippers.

'So I see.'

The endearing sight turned his frown into a smile. He hadn't realised how much he had looked forward to seeing her until she'd opened the door in that ridiculous outfit and immediately lifted his mood.

'I wanted to give you your platter back and thank you again for helping us out. I'm in the doghouse for not inviting you to the party, but I really didn't think a room full of children on a sugar high would be your scene. Anyway, Bastien loved the cake.'

He ruffled his nephew's hair and hoped the cuteness factor would get him off the hook.

Lola took the plate from him with a smile. 'There's no need to worry. As long as the birthday boy was happy, that's all that matters.'

'I *loved* it!' Bastien piped up to give his expert opinion.

'There you go—you'll not get a better recommendation than that.'

There hadn't been much left to clean off the plate. The sumptuous chocolate sponge decorated with colourful sugar dinosaur figures had been delicious as well as a visual feast. Henri had enjoyed two slices and an orange brontosaurus in between games of pass the parcel and musical chairs.

'Did you really make it all yourself?'

Gabrielle hovered beside him, apparently as enthralled by Lola's talents as he was.

'I really did. It's not that hard. All you need is time and patience.'

'Not for me, then?' He didn't have the time to spare on hobbies and had absolutely no patience for sitting still, and he made no apologies for it. His no-nonsense approach to life had got him to the top of his field after all. But it didn't mean he couldn't appreciate a creative spirit such as Lola, whose imagination and eye for detail had put a smile on so many faces.

'Probably not.' Lola peered out at him from beneath lowered lashes, failing to hide her amusement at the very idea.

There was something very endearing about her standing there in her PJs, scrubbed clean of make-up and giving him that shy Princess Diana look. She was the typical girl next door—sweet and innocent, and completely in contrast with the sexy siren he'd seen writhing in that chair at the club. Against his better judgement, he was becoming more and more intrigued by his new member of staff.

'I'd love to try some time.' Gabrielle scuffed her boots on the floor and avoided eye contact with anyone as she voiced her interest.

Unfortunately Henri knew nothing about baking and even less about sugarcraft to be of any use to her. Still, if there was a chance this could improve her mood he'd find a way to make it happen.

'You're welcome to come over any time and I can show you the basics. If that's okay with Henri and your mum?'

Regardless that Lola was saving his bacon for a second time, she was obviously waiting for him to confirm this as a good idea. In terms of avoiding further entanglement with a colleague it was probably the worst thing he could do, but Gabrielle's welfare took priority. What harm could there be in letting her ice a few cakes if it took her mind off whatever ailed her for a few hours?

He held his hand up in surrender, refusing to be an obstacle to his niece's wishes—as per Lola's advice. 'Hey, it's fine by me. I'll run it by Angelique later, but I don't see a problem if it means there's one member of the family who can at least turn the oven on.'

That earned him a chorus of giggles from both children, and he could have hugged Lola for giving Gabrielle something to look forward to. However, throwing his arms around her when she was in her nightwear could be viewed as a tad inappropriate, so he settled for a subtle nod of the head in gratitude instead.

She nodded back. They understood each other. This was for Gabrielle's sake.

'I'm hungry. Have you got any ice cream?' Apparently the moment was lost on Bastien, whose impatience had sent him walking on in to the apartment.

'I'm not sure...' Lola watched, bemused, as he barged past her.

'Sorry about this.' Henri made a grab for his wayward nephew.

'No problem. It's too cold to keep you standing out there anyway. Come in and we can sort out a time for Gabrielle to start her baking masterclass. I'll just put this plate away, then go get changed into something more...mature.'

Lola opened the door wide for him and Gabrielle to enter. If she was inconvenienced by their sudden invasion, good manners covered her tracks. He didn't think *he'd* be so accommodating if she turned up at *his* door with two inquisitive children when he was ready for bed. Although since he slept in the nude that could prove even more awkward.

'Not on my account,' he murmured, quite enjoying this injection of humour into his evening.

It brought another flush of pink to her cheeks before she scurried out of sight.

By the time Henri reached the living room Bastien had already discovered the games console and was busy setting up his favourite racing game.

'Look what she's got, Uncle Henri!' The child's face lit up as he expertly flicked through the set-up screen.

'Her name is Dr Roberts, Bastien, and it's very rude of you to come charging into a lady's house uninvited.'

'But she *did* 'vite us in.'

'Only after you'd made yourself at home. Oh, never mind. Just don't do it again.' Children were exhausting. It was as well he'd decided a long time ago not to have any of his own. Angelique's were a full-time commitment.

Henri took a seat on the leather settee next to Gabrielle,

who sat on the edge with her arms wrapped around her knees. He wished he could wave a magic wand and make her worries disappear.

Lola returned wearing conservative jeans and a fitted floral blouse. Her hair remained the same, though: loose, wavy and free of its ponytail restraint.

'Right. Now that I'm dressed for company, can I get you guys anything to drink?'

'Can I have cola?' Bastien pushed his junk food limits even further.

'You know you're not allowed that. You can have water.' Henri had discovered the after-effects of giving his nephew fizzy drinks before bedtime to his cost. That had been one long night.

'We have fruit juice, too. Gabrielle, would you like some?' Lola came up with a timely alternative, which kept Bastien from further whining.

'Yes, please.'

'Let me give you a hand with the drinks.'

He followed Lola into the kitchen. Whatever spell she'd cast on Gabrielle, he thought they might be able to capitalise on it. If a friendship developed between the pair, there was a chance she might trust Lola with her secrets. All he had to do was convince her to relay any information back to him.

'The glasses are in the top cupboard,' she told him as she yanked the fridge door open.

'Tell me, Dr Roberts, are you moonlighting as an exotic dancer? Don't get me wrong, I'm sure you're worth every penny, but you know the rules about taking paid employment outside of the hospital.'

'Ouch!' Lola banged her head on the top shelf of the fridge. 'Pardon me?'

She lifted out the carton of pure orange juice which had

been pushed to the back in favour of Jules's bottle of Pinot and closed the door.

'I just assumed you must be making extra money somewhere to pay for all this.' He motioned towards all the mod cons Lola took for granted now she wasn't tied to the family's kitchen sink.

'This is Jules's place. I pay rent.'

It seemed she would never be allowed to forget that one night of abandoned dancing at Angelique's burlesque class.

'Ah…'

The devastatingly handsome grin made Lola rue the less-than-flattering bed wear she'd been sporting on his arrival even more. Some people effortlessly exuded sex appeal in their nightwear, while others had all the sophistication of a cartoon pig.

In hindsight, perhaps she should have taken heed of Jules's countless attempts to persuade her to swap her jammies for something more enticing to the opposite sex. She'd resisted those little silk numbers that clung to every curve in favour of shapeless comfort in the belief that no man would ever get close enough for it to matter.

Since Henri had shown up uninvited, and practically stared through her fleecy protective layer, she might have to change her view. Especially when that appreciative gaze had warmed her insides rather than freaked her out.

Lola shooed away the mental image of standing before him in one of those provocative outfits that mocked her every time she walked through the lingerie department on her way to Matching Separates. She didn't want to associate him with a need to feel attractive. He was her boss, Gabrielle's uncle, and a man in whom she couldn't afford to invest any feelings.

Perhaps all this confidence-building was starting to pay off and she was beginning to function as a warm-blooded human, no longer tied to her *victim* roots. She hoped so.

Not because she had any intention of fostering an attraction to her boss, but because she wanted to feel like any other twenty-five-year-old single woman, who could engage with a good-looking man without having a meltdown.

'Okay, so there's no more confusion, I can categorically state I'm *not* a stripper.'

'And I'm not father to a teenage girl—or anyone else for that matter. What age did you think I was anyway?'

Henri let his ego peek out at the idea that he could be perceived as anything other than a young, eligible bachelor. It was an invitation for Lola to get her own back.

She screwed her face up, as though she was really struggling with the idea that he wasn't an old fogey. 'Umm... eighty-five? Eighty-six?'

'Very funny.'

'Seriously, though, you have such a good way with the children, I'm sure I'm not the only one to have made that mistake. Obviously, it would've made you a teenage dad...'

'Obviously.'

Lola poured juice into the tumblers lined up on the marble work surface and slid one over to him. 'How are things with Gabrielle at the minute, Doctor?'

'Henri.'

'Pardon?'

'I've gatecrashed your quiet night in, and my nephew is probably destroying your living room as we speak, so I think you could drop the formalities and call me Henri.'

'Okay, *Henri*.' It sounded weird to say his Christian name out loud, as though they had some sort of personal relationship going on. Which they didn't, of course, outside of concern for his niece's welfare.

Henri cleared his throat and watched his juice as he swirled it in the glass. 'I'd be lying if I said I wasn't concerned about her.'

'No progress, then?' It was worrying when a girl that

age shut herself off. Lola knew how quickly loneliness and despair spiralled into something more sinister. At least Gabrielle had a mother and a father figure to support her through whatever was going on. All it would take was a little trust for her to open up to them.

'She locks herself in her room all night and barely eats. I was surprised when she agreed to come with me tonight, but she seems genuinely interested in this new hobby. Thanks for offering your services—it's very much appreciated. I have another big favour to ask you, though. If she tells you anything that could help us get to the bottom of this, will you please pass it on?'

The impassioned plea was difficult to ignore when there was a pair of big brown eyes accompanying it. Gabrielle's behaviour didn't sound any different from that of a certain junior doctor, and Lola was starting to see why her brothers were on her case so much. It came from a place of love. Both she and Gabrielle were lucky to have such caring families, even if they were too close to see it for themselves.

'It's down to Gabrielle if she wants to talk about it. I'm certainly not going to push the subject and make her think we're somehow tricking her. But be assured I want to help wherever I can.'

Lola understood Henri's desire to find out the truth at all costs, but she also needed Gabrielle to feel safe here. For her, baking was a way to escape everything negative in her life, and she wanted it to be the same for her new protégée.

Although his frown was ploughing grooves into his forehead, Henri didn't argue with her.

'I'm hungry.' The young boy, whose strong Belfast accent differed so greatly from his uncle's, appeared at the kitchen door. 'You got somethin' to eat?'

He did, however, have the Frenchman's directness.

'We'll go soon, Bastien. Sorry—I promised to take them for fried chicken.' Henri grimaced and set down his glass.

'And ice cream?' Bastien reminded him.

'*And* ice cream.'

Henri winked, and Lola marvelled at his relaxed relationship with the child. If anything, he was a push-over with these kids, and this visit showed he would do anything for them—including sacrifice his pride to ask her for help. Despite her initial impression, Henri was a nice guy after all.

Bastien clapped his hands and reminded her that he was present—and hungry. An idea formed in her head to accommodate his needs *and* those of his sister.

'Fried chicken and ice cream sounds yummy. You know *I* haven't had any dinner yet, either.'

Henri picked up the ball and ran with it. 'Would you like to join us?'

'I would *love* to. Why don't you and Bastien go and fetch the food whilst Gabrielle and I set the table?'

Bastien ran off to share the news with his sister.

'It will give me a chance to talk to her,' she explained somewhat unnecessarily to Henri.

At least this way any prying now wouldn't sully their baking time in the future.

'I know. *Merci beaucoup.*'

Henri kissed her on the cheek, and just like that the touch of his surprisingly soft lips on her skin short-circuited all her anti-hunk defence systems.

Once Henri and Bastien had left, there was an air of expectancy between the girls for the conversation they needed to have. But Lola wanted to ask questions in a way that wouldn't frighten her off. She held the cutlery out to Gabrielle, as if she was trying to coax a skittish animal out of hiding with some food.

'How's the eye?' She carried on arranging the placemats on the table to prevent her concern from seeming like a big deal.

'Fine.' As before, Gabrielle kept her head down so her hair fell across her face.

Lola knew that trick. She'd used it countless times to hide from her brothers' prying eyes.

'You know you can talk to me if there's anything bothering you? Sometimes it's easier to tell a friend your problems than family. They're not as emotionally involved, and therefore tend not to rant as much.'

'Thanks.' The young girl lifted her head to afford her a half smile but her eyes were glassy with tears. Whatever her burden, she had clearly found no relief since their meeting at the hospital.

'I had a few "accidents" in high school myself—falling over people's feet and into their fists. It's all I can do these days not to slap those who tell you that your schooldays are the best days of your life.'

'Ha!'

The teenager's vocal outburst echoed Lola's thoughts on the subject.

'Exactly. I couldn't wait to leave. If I'd believed that was as good as my life would get I'd never have made it out.'

She'd had more than her inner turmoil to escape in high school, but it was important that Gabrielle knew there was light at the end of the tunnel if she was experiencing the same problems.

'And things *did* get better?'

Her interest sparked, Gabrielle halted her arrangement of the knives and forks. It gave Lola more than a hint that she'd touched on the right nerve.

'They did. I'm happy now.' Although she still bore the mental scars, if not the physical ones.

Gabrielle's sigh didn't sound as though she was convinced.

'I know things may seem insurmountable now, but in the grand scheme of things I'm sure they're not as bad as you imagine.' Lola had gone through some horrific times—to the point where she hadn't wanted to wake up in the mornings. But she'd fought through and come out the other side a better person than those who'd tormented her.

'Right now they're pretty bad.'

The soft voice made more impact on Lola than tears ever could. It was the sound of someone who'd already accepted defeat.

Lola could play twenty questions again, and get no further, or go with her gut feeling about the matter. Gabrielle was a beautiful girl with an exotic mother. People had a tendency to find fault with anything out of the norm, and Henri's niece was sensitive enough to take criticism to heart. Teenage girls—and boys—could be unforgivably cruel.

'Is there someone in school giving you a hard time?'

It would explain the truancy, as well as the mood. Lola had skipped her fair share of classes to avoid those making her life a misery. She'd had to put in a hell of a lot of hard work at home, to catch up on the lessons she'd missed, but it had been easier than listening to cruel taunts and mocking laughter.

Gabrielle's silence was deafening.

'In another few years those people and their opinions won't matter. You'll probably never see or think about them again.'

The white lie was for the girl's benefit. Lola doubted there was any point in telling her she spent a good chunk of her life reliving the nightmare over again. Gabrielle came across as a stronger personality than the young Lola had ever been, and there was every possibility she would find it easier to move on after high school if they could resolve the issue quickly.

'You have a bright future ahead of you. Don't let small-minded bullies prevent you from reaching your potential. The more school you miss, the harder it will be to catch up. And I'm speaking from experience.'

She'd be a lot further along in her career by now if she'd lived by her own words. Those years she'd wasted living in perpetual fear would never be recovered, no matter how hard she tried.

'You probably think I'm being stupid, but I just can't face it any more. They tell everyone who'll listen that my mum's a stripper, and that I must be adopted because I'm so ugly. Even if I don't see them in school they send me text messages and say horrible things over the internet.'

Gabrielle's shoulders sagged under the weight of the abuse, and her eyes brimmed with sorrow.

Lola swallowed the lump in her throat and tried to retain her composure. It wouldn't do to swamp the girl in an overemotional hug.

She wasn't sure knowing the truth made the situation any easier. It was no wonder Gabrielle couldn't confide in her family. Angelique would be horrified to find out *she* was the cause of her daughter's suffering, and Henri might well use the information to stop his sister doing what she loved. Knowledge could be a dangerous weapon, and Lola had managed to land herself with a ticking time bomb.

Gabrielle sniffed, and reminded Lola that her welfare was the most important part of the equation. 'I would urge you to speak to your mum or your uncle—they're really worried about you. You should really let the school know what's happening, too, so they can put a stop to it.'

It was easier said than done, of course. In Lola's case teachers and family had only made matters worse and marked her as a target. She didn't even know how she could aid Gabrielle, short of being a shoulder to lean on.

Gabrielle shook her head violently. 'It'll only make things worse. You don't understand…'

'I've been there, sweetheart. I was a bit of a tomboy when I was young. Not really by choice. My dad raised me the same way he raised my brothers. I may as well have been his fourth son—it was no wonder I attracted negative attention. If these people are allowed to get away with picking on you, things will never get better for you.'

Sharing the horrors of her childhood had never been therapeutic for Lola—it simply reawakened that demon of dread in the pit of her stomach. She'd only opened up for Gabrielle's sake, so she knew there was someone who understood.

'It shouldn't matter where you come from, who you are or what you look like. People should be free to be whoever they are.' Gabrielle folded her arms across her chest and mirrored her feisty mother.

'I agree. Unfortunately there will always be those who revel in making other people's lives hell.'

'What did they do to you?'

Given her lineage, Gabrielle's directness shouldn't have come as a shock.

For her own sake—and Gabrielle's—Lola filtered out the most appalling aspects of her teen years. 'They teased me that they weren't sure if I was a boy or a girl.'

Any attack on a girl's appearance at such a vulnerable age would dent anyone's confidence. Especially at a time when popularity and boyfriends had seemed the most important things in the world and her friends had been pairing off to leave her as the odd one out. Placing value on those things had cost her so much.

'But you're *beautiful*.'

The compliment thrown Lola's way was appreciated, but she would never get used to receiving praise without thinking there was an ulterior motive. Her trust had been smashed to smithereens in one summer afternoon, never again to be given freely.

'And if I told you *you're* beautiful would you believe me?' Lola turned the tables back, doing her best to illustrate how skewed self-esteem became in these situations.

'No.' She glaned up at Lola from beneath lowered lids, every bit as cynical as she.

'For the record, you are *gorgeous*.' Lola cupped Gabrielle's face in her hands and tilted her head up. She wanted to look her in the eye as she said it, willing her to believe. 'But it's more to do with how you feel about yourself, isn't it?'

Gabrielle bit her lip to stop it from wobbling.

'I know it's difficult, but don't give those cowards power over you. Be strong.' Lola's words caught in her throat. She could easily have been talking to her younger self. In reality, it had taken years for her to heed that advice.

'I'm fed up with being strong. I just want to forget about everything.' Stress furrowed her youthful brow.

Lola recognised the destructive nature of those locked-in emotions. The spectre of suicide had haunted the deprived council estate where she had grown up. Teenagers ravaged by the effects of drugs and alcohol, or those who just hadn't seen a way out of poverty, had taken their own lives on a shockingly regular basis. It was only seeing the devastation of the families left in the aftermath which had prevented Lola from seeking the same escape when her life had become unbearable.

Even though some of those issues plagued her still, Lola was glad she'd fought for the life she had today, and she would do everything to ensure someone in similar circumstances would get that second chance, too.

'There's nothing that can take your mind off your troubles better than a homemade cake.'

She'd done as Henri had asked and knew when to back off. At least they'd made a start on talks, even if they had yet to come up with an effective solution to Gabrielle's problems. It was clear that what this child needed was some fun to take her mind off everything—and that she could definitely help with.

'I can't wait.' Thankfully Gabrielle had now swapped her despair for a grin.

'We will bake up a storm in here as soon your mum gives the go-ahead. Who knows? Maybe we can get her involved, too?'

As keen as she was to have a cake buddy, she didn't want to interfere in what should be a mother/daughter bonding exercise.

The doorbell rang and sent Gabrielle scurrying back into her shell. 'Promise you won't say anything to Uncle Henri?'

She was putting Lola in a very tricky position. Henri was her superior, and he would be actively looking for answers regarding his niece's welfare. However, facing his temper against the consequences of betraying Gabrielle was the lesser of two evils. The child needed someone to confide in, someone to trust. As did Lola.

'I promise. When you're ready you can tell him yourself.'

The buzzer went again, and again, until she was forced to answer the door in case the neighbours complained about the noise.

'I'll bet you anything that's Bastien.' Gabrielle finished setting the table and carefully arranged her emotions back in order.

No good could ever come to someone afraid to express their feelings. At some point that bottled-up anger and sorrow would erupt into an almighty mess. It made Lola's decision to stay loyal to Gabrielle that much easier.

'Bastien, take your finger off the doorbell, please.' An unamused Henri sounded on the other side of the door.

She found him juggling takeaway bags and a mischievous child.

'Someone's impatient.' Lola took one of the bags off his hands as Bastien dashed inside.

'Sorry.' Henri shrugged as he lost control of his nephew again. 'I guess nothing stands in the way of a boy and his fast food.'

'I guess not.' Lola wished some of that devil-may-care attitude would rub off on his sister.

Henri walked back into the apartment as though this was an everyday occurrence for him. In fact this whole thing was surreal. He never imagined he'd find himself asking anyone for help regarding his family. Especially someone he hardly knew. Someone he wasn't even sure was up to the job. Yet here he was, eating takeaway with her and praying she could fix his niece.

'Did she tell you anything?' he asked Lola as they unpacked the cartons in the kitchen.

'She didn't go into details, but I think we're making progress.' Lola kept her back to him as she plated the food.

'So she told you *something*?' He didn't want Lola holding all the cards. This wasn't *her* family. All that was required from her was to pass on the information and let him deal with it.

'I swore to keep everything confidential, Henri. I'm sorry.' Lola tried to bustle past him.

As if he would be willing to leave it there. He sidestepped to block her path and forced her to look at him.

'Don't do this to me, Lola. I feel helpless enough without you holding back on me, too.' He kept his voice low, imploring her to see things from his point of view.

'I'm sorry. I promised.'

'At least tell me if I have anything to be worried about.' He couldn't help but wonder if she enjoyed having this power over him. After all, he was now at her mercy.

Lola raised her eyes to the ceiling and sighed. 'If at any time I don't think I can deal with this on my own I will let you know. For now, I think it's better Gabrielle works through this the way she wants.'

'She's my niece—my responsibility. She shouldn't be going through this on her own.'

If he had his own way he would wrap her up in cotton wool and protect her from everything negative in the world. He was the only consistent male role model in her life. And what use was he if he couldn't help her in her hour of need?

'The food's going cold.' Lola pursed her lips. She could be stubborn when the mood took her.

'I don't give a damn about the food. I want to talk about *this*.'

'What you want isn't always the most important thing in the world. The sooner you learn that the better.'

With a burst of bravado, Lola pushed past him and carried the dinner into the living room.

When he did finally take his seat at the table he was forced to turn his frown upside down. Bastien was revelling in eating his chicken with his fingers, leaving grease and breadcrumbs everywhere. Gabrielle's laughter at her little brother's caveman manners was a glorious sound.

Lola was right. It was progress. He was going to have to defer to her on the subject of his niece. However much it galled him.

CHAPTER FOUR

As Lola made her way to the hospital the next morning her mind was less preoccupied with work than with her personal issues. There was no doubt that sharing her experiences with Gabrielle had been the key to getting the teenager to open up, but it had cost her a night without sleep. Nightmares and tears over those dark days, and worry over keeping Gabrielle's secrets from Henri, had kept her awake. Yet it would all be worth it to prevent Gabrielle any further pain.

If she didn't want the school or her mother involved, then all Lola could do was offer her friendship. Perhaps if *she'd* had someone to turn to, life mightn't have seemed so bleak to her back then.

Lola went about her rounds, treating fractures and poorly patients without incident, the distraction of work good for settling her nerves.

As she power-walked down the corridor, she encountered Henri for the first time since their impromptu dinner. A meal which had come to a surly end after she'd refused to divulge any information about his niece. Poor Bastien had been forced to eat his ice cream much more quickly than he would have liked.

As they marched towards each other she braced herself for another attempt to break her loyalty. She nodded an acknowledgement and Henri grunted something unintelligible as he strode past. Whilst she didn't want another guilt trip about keeping him out of the loop, this was plain childishness.

She pivoted around. 'I appreciate how frustrating it is for you, under the circumstances, but I'm sure Gabrielle will come to you when she's ready. Snubbing me at work, however, is ridiculous. Surely we're adult enough to separate our personal issues from our professional lives?'

When she said 'we', she meant *you*. He needed to realise that she wasn't required to jump at every click of his fingers. No doubt his control freakery was part of the reason Gabrielle didn't want him involved. One whiff of the goings-on and he would be at the school, sandblasting everyone he came into contact with. In Lola's opinion the matter needed handling with kid gloves—not a sledgehammer.

He did a heart-stoppingly slow U-turn to face her. 'I am trying to keep the matter private. That is why I hadn't intended discussing it in the middle of the corridor. I'm grateful for your help with my niece, but do not use that as an excuse to undermine my authority at work.'

Another one-hundred-and-eighty-degree turn and he took off, leaving Lola with her mouth hanging open wide enough to fit both feet in. When would she ever learn that she and good-looking men simply didn't mix?

'Can you take this one for me? I'm run off my feet.' Jules offloaded a file into her hands as soon as she walked into the department.

'Sure.' Lola's heart sank as she scanned the case notes, but she didn't have the option of saying no. This was her job, and she was going to have to treat all patients equally—regardless of age or gender.

She paused outside the cubicle and took a deep breath. The way her heart seemed to be lurching into her throat one might have been forgiven for thinking she'd never

been alone with a man before. It was the actions of a few
who'd caused her to distrust the rest.

'Okay, Mr...Smith. I see you've been in the wars today.'

A man in his mid-twenties was lying bare-chested, his
face and jeans covered in blood and dirt. With his once
blond hair matted red, and the area around his right eye
a beautiful shade of violet, he was a painfully colourful
sight.

'I walked into a door,' he said with a smirk.

He'd clearly been on the receiving end of someone's
fist, but Lola didn't argue. All she had to do was patch him
up and get him out. She leaned in to clean away the blood
and find the source. The smell of stale cigarettes and beer
assaulted her, taking her back to another time and place.

Think of somewhere safe...someone safe.

As she dabbed at the cuts on his scalp and face with
cotton wool she imagined Henri beside her, despite their
recent difference of opinion. She could almost smell his
clean fragrance, so reassuring and familiar. It gave her the
push to carry on.

'I think you need a couple of stitches. Nothing serious.'

Once she'd cleaned the wound in order to start suturing, she became aware of her patient's eyes almost burning into her.

'Do I know you from somewhere?'

'I don't think so.'

She withdrew her hand as it began to shake. It wouldn't
do to send a patient out with crooked stitches.

'I'm sure I've seen your face before.'

He propped himself up on his elbows to peer at her,
crossing so far into her personal space his breath prick-
led her skin.

'I get that a lot.'

A step back to deposit the soiled cotton balls in the
wastebin meant she could breathe again.

'I *know* you.'

He was up off the bed before she could react, pinning her into the corner of the tiny cubicle. 'We went to the same high school.'

Lola gasped for air as her throat closed over. This was her worst nightmare come true—being confronted with her past with no obvious means of escape.

'You're mistaken. Now, if you'll climb back onto the bed, we'll get those stitches finished so you can go on your way.'

'I remember you. Lola Roberts.'

His revolting sneer confirmed that he'd witnessed the horrendous incident in her teens, maybe even been part of it.

He moved closer. She stepped back until she hit herself against the trolley.

'Please…'

It was a plea for him to stop. The same pathetic voice she'd used ten years ago. It hadn't worked then, either.

He ran a hand along her arm and her goose-pimpled flesh reacted violently against it, despite the barrier of her white coat.

'You're *definitely* all woman now, Lola.'

In her mind's eye she could envisage that sea of faces staring at her, feel the hands holding her down, hear their drunken jeers ringing in her ears as she sobbed. This time she would scream for all she was worth if it came to it. She'd worked hard to overcome that paralysing fear—this was her chance to finally lay some demons to rest.

'You can either sit back down and let me finish your treatment, Mr *Smith*, or I can call Security.'

A strategic crossing of her arms shrugged him off and hid her shaking limbs at the same time.

He narrowed his eyes at her. 'Don't get all uppity, now, Doctor. You're no better than me. I can still picture you, with your DIY haircut and secondhand clothes. If I remember well, you weren't so high and mighty when you were lying on the floor with your underwear pulled down.'

Lola's eyes burned with tears and memories, but she wouldn't let those bullies continue to have power over her.

'You were there that night? Perhaps I can pass on your details to the police. They're still looking for witnesses and accomplices to the sexual assault of a minor.'

It was a lie, of course. The incident had gone unreported since her brothers had taken the law into their own hands and risked being arrested themselves. The handsome rugby captain who'd lured her into the trap had taken quite a few weeks to heal after the beating he'd taken, and Lola had left the school soon after that fateful night.

However, the threat of police involvement was enough to make her patient turn pale and get him to back off. The sense of power and relief at finding her voice again made her question why she didn't start *every* day by kicking some arrogant male ass.

That immediately brought a certain frosty registrar to mind. Henri was the perfect sparring partner—strong enough to boost her ego when she got a verbal win against him, intimidating without ever being a threat. A lot of her anxieties about him had been laid to rest since seeing the way he was with his niece and nephew. Behind the grouchy outer shell there was a loving man with a heart of gold.

She ignored the thought about kicking his ass. It wouldn't do to linger on how cute it was when she was seeing more of him than her own family at the minute.

Unfortunately her lapse in concentration was an open invitation for a predator like Smith. He clamped his hand around her elbow and jolted her back into the present danger.

'If you know what's good for you, you'll keep me out of it. Right?'

She refused to let the mask slip and tried not to react to the fingers digging into her skin—or the inner voice telling her to knee him where it hurt and run. A big part of this job was keeping calm in the face of adversity, and it didn't come more adversarial than physical assault.

'Take. Your. Hands. Off. Me.'

She maintained eye contact, kept her voice steady, even though every part of her was screaming either to karate chop him away or crumple to the floor. If she ever wanted to succeed and shake off the demons of her past she would have to front this out. This was a test of her courage and an indicator of how far she'd come in the past couple of years. One immature thug wasn't going to break her now.

'You're needed at Reception, Dr Roberts. I can deal with this.'

Henri barged in and the grip on her arm immediately relaxed. Mr Smith was decidedly less intimidating with someone bigger and stronger on the scene.

Although Henri's presence had changed the oppressive atmosphere in the cubicle, Lola wasn't thrilled at his interference. If she wanted Gabrielle to stand strong it was important that she lead by example and not rely on someone else coming to her rescue.

'I'm almost done here.'

'They need you *now*. I'm sure your patient won't mind if I take over.' He didn't give either of them a choice, bustling in to prep for suturing.

The story didn't quite add up. Why would anyone be so desperate for a first year's expertise over a registrar's? No doubt he thought she'd been taking too long with what was a minor injury. If he'd bothered to give her a chance to explain the delay in private he would have realised seeing this through to the end was more important to her than waiting times.

'If you insist.'

Not so long ago she'd have gladly deferred to her superior, but Mr Stompy-Boots had marched over her progress a second time. It was like taking one step forward and getting rugby tackled to the ground before ever reaching the touchline. For Henri's sake, this had better not be about his personal issues with her. Now that her inner badass was getting airtime, if he wasn't careful he'd find himself next on the list for a piece of her mind.

Her body shook with suppressed rage and residual fear. She didn't know which of the two men had done her more damage in the past few minutes. It was only the fact that she was physically and emotionally exhausted that put an end to her fight.

Henri waited until Lola had left and he knew she was safe before turning on the lowlife who'd had his paws all over her. She'd held her ground, but he'd seen the terror in her eyes as someone nearly twice her size had her cornered with no obvious means of escape.

He'd only come down to apologise for the way he'd spoken to her earlier. After he'd had time to dwell on his behaviour he'd realised he should be working to keep her onside for the sake of his niece. As he'd waited outside the cubicle, trying to form adequate words to express his regret, he'd heard part of the conversation going on inside. Enough to prompt him to get her the hell out of there.

Sexual assault of a minor?

It didn't bear thinking about that she'd been a victim of such a serious crime, and thus it came as no wonder that she had a tendency to be wary of others. Someone had stolen her trust, her innocence, and here she was working to help others.

Lola was braver than he'd given her credit for. He'd burdened her with his personal problems without a thought for her own, even though since day one he'd pegged her as the weak link in an otherwise dynamic group of ambitious new doctors. Now not only was she his student, she was his family counsellor—someone he'd come to count on as his friend.

It tore him apart that he hadn't been able to prevent her from being hurt. Since no one had apparently been charged there seemed little he could do now except be there for her and play the role of protector that he'd perfected over the years.

As he approached the patient he was duty-bound to treat, Henri's hands weren't as steady as they should have been with the needle. In his opinion Mr Smith didn't deserve any compassion, and he'd be lucky if he didn't leave with more injuries than he'd arrived with. But despite his personal feelings Henri knew his career depended upon him being a professional at all times.

'Oww!'

A professional whose bedside manner had a tendency to slip now and again.

He closed the wound efficiently and without finesse. 'You'll need to come back in a few days to have the stitches removed.'

Henri leaned in until he was nose to nose with Lola's patient, taking some delight in turning the tables as the other man backed up against the pillows.

'Make sure you ask for me. There's no need for you to disturb Dr Roberts again. Do you understand?'

If people insisted on labelling him as intimidating, he'd use it to his advantage when called for.

There was no response.

'Perhaps we should involve the police after all. We both know your injuries weren't sustained by accident. I suspect men like you have a habit of getting on the wrong side of people. I can make the call now, if you'd like?'

Henri stuffed his hand in the pocket of his trousers to retrieve his phone.

Smith scrambled to his feet and whipped the curtain
back, showing more fear than Lola ever had. 'It's no skin
off my nose. She's still a freak.'

Bare-chested, he crawled back to whatever hole he'd
slunk out of. It wouldn't end there, as far as Henri was
concerned. Even with only partial knowledge of what had
happened before he'd arrived on the scene, he wouldn't rest
until he knew the full story and found out what he could
do to help Lola.

'You had no right to do that.'

Lola ambushed him the minute he set foot back in his
office. Henri should have known she wouldn't take kindly
to being sent on a wild goose chase to some non-existent
emergency. But one look at her arms wrapped around her
waist in a self-conscious hug and he knew he'd made the
right call.

'I want to know what happened, Lola. I'm as responsible for my junior doctors as I am for my patients. You
don't have to put up with anyone trying to make you uncomfortable when you're trying to do your job.'

His interference was a common source of discontent
amongst all the womenfolk in his life. But after what he'd
overheard he deemed it justifiable on this occasion.

'*Trying* to do my job? Admit it—this is about your lack
of belief in my abilities as a doctor. You don't think I have
what it takes, but I *will* prove you wrong. Difficult situations are part of the learning process, and I won't get anywhere if you keep jumping in to bail me out.'

She made no reference to the deeply personal aspect
of the confrontation, but he could see the trauma of it reflected in those expressive sea-green eyes. If this was only
about her journey into the world of medicine he would

agree—the best thing for him to do *would* be to back off. After all, getting her to step up to the plate was what he'd wanted from the start. But this was about keeping her safe.

He toyed with the idea of dropping the subject altogether, to save her from further discomfort, but she was the one who'd made the passionate plea about Gabrielle needing someone to talk to about her problems. And Henri hadn't got his reputation from tiptoeing around people's feelings.

'I heard what you said. About the police.'

'It's not your concern.'

She stood firm, as obstinate as his sister and niece. Such independent spirit made it difficult for a man to be gallant without being accused of tyranny.

'When one of my staff is accosted in my department it becomes very much my concern, *chérie*. Were you hurt?' He balled his fists as his protective streak reared its ugly head.

'I told you—I was handling it.'

'I mean before. The assault.'

Even saying it left a bad taste in his mouth. He couldn't begin to imagine how it made Lola feel. She flinched, and he hated himself for making her relive it.

'No. I wasn't physically harmed, but I was humiliated… I really don't want to discuss this with anyone.' Lola shook her head and the tears sitting like dew on her eyelashes spilled down her face.

It came naturally for Henri to go and put an arm around her shoulders. Despite his outward appearance, he was still a tactile Frenchman at heart.

'If you need closure you can still press charges. I'll support you.'

Lola made a hiccupping sound as she swallowed a sob. 'I don't need your pity. Yes, things happened, and I had a hard time moving past them for a while, but that has no bearing on my training. If anything, I've become a stronger person for it. Not that it is any of your business.'

'As my niece is none of *yours*. Yet I understand your involvement is best for her welfare.'

He wanted her to take her own advice and let someone in. Despite the mention of her older brothers, he got the impression Lola was someone who preferred to work through her problems herself. He could empathise with that. Not once had he confided in anyone about the burden of guilt he carried over Angelique's failed medical career. It didn't mean it was healthy.

'The difference is that you came to me for help with Gabrielle. I, on the other hand, can fight my own battles.'

She was so determined to prove her strength she didn't even wipe away her tears. As though denying their existence would render them invisible.

He brushed the two telltale signs of her distress away with the pads of his thumbs. Although he couldn't say it without sounding like a patronising ass, he was proud of her.

'I have no doubt about that. I just want you to know that I care about you.'

At this moment in time someone needed to tell her that, show her that, and remind her she wasn't alone.

He'd only intended to give her a friendly peck on the lips—not too far removed from the double cheek-kiss greeting he exchanged with his sister or his fellow countrymen. Except kissing Lola definitely wasn't the platonic gesture he'd imagined.

Her mouth was soft and yielding beneath his, and he couldn't resist dipping inside to taste her sweetness. She met him with a tentative nudge of her tongue and Henri was lost. With her head cradled in his hands, he deepened the kiss, every primitive urge he had rising above his good intentions.

Only when she stiffened against him did common sense prevail. He sprang away from her, eager for her to put back those barriers that he'd so stupidly breached.

'I'm so sorry, Lola.'

He raked his hands through his hair, repenting his sins immediately. All he'd done was compound her fears that no man could be trusted. Kissing her when she was vulnerable and frightened made him no better than the sleaze who'd accosted her in the first place.

It was no wonder she was frozen to the spot, those big green eyes wide and alert. He'd broken her trust in a moment of madness, with no rhyme or reason behind his actions except for pure, unadulterated lust. Inexcusable behaviour—and, apart from every other personal violation against Lola, most definitely a sackable offence. He'd screwed up big time and all he could do was beg for her forgiveness.

'This is entirely on me. I got carried away. You know I would never do anything to hurt you.'

He cringed at the words—probably used the world over to excuse a multitude of sins against women. In this case he meant them with every fibre of his being.

The only thing that unnerved him more than his loss of control was Lola's silence. It was no surprise that she'd shut herself off, since he'd heaped one violation on top of another. He was her superior, supposedly her friend, and he had no business laying a finger on her no matter what the circumstances.

'Lola, talk to me—hit me. Do something so I know you're okay.'

If it wouldn't have compounded the offence he would have shaken her. She was scaring the hell out of him. Had he pushed her over the edge into some sort of delayed shock? Post-traumatic stress wouldn't be unusual in such cases. He desperately needed her to come back into the room and leave wherever it was she'd gone in her head.

'I have to go.'

Those four little words as she blinked back at him and slowly returned to her body were enough for Henri to breathe a sigh of relief. Yet they weren't enough to stop him worrying as she left in a trance-like state. He wouldn't go after her—he'd done enough damage—but he would make sure to send someone to check on her.

Other than Lola, the only person who could possibly hate him more than he hated himself right now would be Gabrielle. With one selfish move he'd destroyed not one but two budding relationships.

CHAPTER FIVE

'I'M REALLY SORRY. Gabrielle was so looking forward to seeing you, and Angelique is at Bastien's parent/teacher evening at the school. I couldn't get hold of you to check this was still okay.'

Henri hovered on Lola's doorstep, almost using Gabrielle as a shield in front of him. Of *course* he hadn't been able to get her permission for a visit, since she'd avoided all forms of attempted communication from him. There were dozens of unread texts on her phone, and calls that she hadn't been able to bring herself to answer. She knew beyond all doubt how sorry he was about kissing her. The trouble was she couldn't fully fathom how *she* felt about it.

'You said you'd show me the basics…'

Gabrielle fidgeted with her braid and guilt-tripped Lola over her reluctance to let Henri get close stand in the way of her promise.

In truth, it was her own actions she was worried about— not his. He'd surprised her with that kiss. She'd had no idea he'd ever looked at her as anything other than a pain in his backside. Perhaps he'd simply felt sorry for her? Whatever the cause, it had made her question how she saw *him*. There was definitely an attraction there. An unwanted one.

'Maybe we should leave. If you'd prefer, you and

Gabrielle can make arrangements for another time and her mother will accompany her in future?'

Now Henri was being the reasonable one. And she couldn't avoid him for ever when they worked at the same hospital—in the same department, for goodness' sake. Besides, what had gone on between them wasn't Gabrielle's fault, and she shouldn't be punished for it.

'Not at all. Come in.'

This evening was about having fun with Gabrielle. Everything else could wait.

'Phone me when you want me to pick her up.'

With his head down and shoulders slumped, Henri turned to leave.

Gabrielle faltered once she saw he was leaving. 'Aren't you coming in, too, Uncle Henri?'

Although she hadn't wanted to discuss anything in front of him, it was only natural she should want him nearby. Lola didn't want to upset her by sending him away and leaving Gabrielle with someone who was pretty much a stranger to her.

Henri halted, waiting for instruction. It put Lola's mind at ease that he wouldn't push her into anything she didn't feel equipped to deal with right now. If he could sit in a corner somewhere, without uttering one word in that accent that should come with a health warning, they might make it through the evening without any more drama.

'You're very welcome to stay, Henri,' she said, her breath hitching even as she invited him in.

This was a different kind of fear than she'd ever known before—an excitement about the unknown rather than the paralysing wait at another's mercy.

His face relaxed into a smile and he mouthed 'Thank you' as he brushed past her. Even that small contact sent a surge of electricity zapping across her skin. Evidently that one kiss had stirred a passion she hadn't even known was still there after everything she'd been through.

The timing couldn't have been worse. After all her hard work to get where she was today, she didn't want to jeopardise it by falling for her boss. It was only asking for trouble with a man like Henri.

She closed the door behind her visitors and took a deep breath. It was time to act her age and not be some shy teenage version of herself.

'I was hoping we could start with cupcakes?'

Gabrielle bit her lip, as if she was worried she was making an outrageous demand.

'With the fuss you were making about coming over here I thought we were dealing with an emergency,' Henri said dryly.

Lola got the impression there'd been quite a discussion between uncle and niece before they'd rocked up at her apartment. No doubt Henri had tried to talk Gabrielle out of going ahead with this, in order to avoid the woman he'd kissed without permission, and it would have taken a great deal on the young girl's part to stand up for what she wanted.

Lola didn't want either of them to regret the decision they'd made in the end.

'It's no problem, Henri. I offered to show her. Besides, the need for cake is most *definitely* an emergency.'

It was cool. They'd managed to be in the same room for five minutes already without anyone getting kissed or being overemotional. She would take Gabrielle into the kitchen and disappear behind a cloud of flour and icing sugar.

'If you're sure…?'

'I am. Now, you make yourself at home and Gabrielle and I will go bake up a storm.'

She met his eyes, assuring him that events hadn't

changed her desire to befriend his niece. Other more delicate matters could be worked out at a later date. When she understood herself how to resolve them.

Once Gabrielle was kitted out in an apron, to protect her designer hoodie from the ravages of margarine and eggs, Lola set her to work fetching basic ingredients.

'So, it's cupcakes you want?'

At least this was one area she was confident in. Those years of trying to feed four hungry men on a tiny budget hadn't been wasted—she could turn her hand to most things in the kitchen.

'Can we try chocolate ones? Uncle Henri always buys them for us as a special treat, but I'd love to learn how to make them myself. Any that Mum makes are usually either burnt or chewy.' Gabrielle screwed up her nose in disgust as she bore witness to her mother's crimes against baked goods.

So Henri had a sweet tooth? She'd had him down as more of a savoury type of guy. With any luck she could feed him cake until he was too full to move or even speak for the rest of the night.

'Chocolate cupcakes it is, then. I'll get the paper cases and you can make a start on weighing everything out.'

It was probably the easiest recipe for Gabrielle to follow herself, and any boost to her confidence, no matter how small, was a bonus.

'How are things at school?'

Lola had shown her how to mix the batter and waited until she was distracted before unleashing the question. Gabrielle had made the point that she simply wanted to hang out tonight, but it wouldn't hurt to find out how the ground lay.

'Okay...'

She was concentrating so hard on creaming the fat and sugar together she didn't seem spooked at the question.

Lola pushed her a tad further. 'Okay, good, or okay, the same?'

Gabrielle shrugged. 'The same. Do I add the eggs and flour now?'

'Yes. Fold them in gently with the cocoa powder, and when you have a nice smooth batter you can spoon it into the cases.'

Lola knew the change of subject was the equivalent of Gabrielle hiding behind her hair, so she tried a different tactic.

'I had an interesting time at work the other day. I had to treat one of the guys who made my life hell in school.'

Cake mixture dripped from the spoon as Gabrielle stood transfixed by the story. 'What happened?'

Lola put herself under pressure not to reveal the terror she'd still felt after all these years. This had to be a story about overcoming those fears and giving Gabrielle hope.

'Well, even though he tried to make me feel small, I dug deep and found the courage to stand up to him. That's the thing, Gabrielle—these people will always be immature and short-sighted, while we grow and develop.'

She omitted the part about Henri interrupting her breakthrough moment, since it spoiled the whole moral of her story. She didn't have to take abuse from anybody at any age.

'Wow. How did it feel?'

Gabrielle's eyes had nearly popped out of her head, she was so enthralled with the idea of giving those bullies a taste of their own medicine. Lola had to admit her reaction gave her a warm fuzzy feeling inside. It confirmed her view that she was becoming the confident professional she was supposed to be and not the simpering helpless damsel Henri seemed to think she was.

'Bloody brilliant. I thoroughly recommend it.'

She revelled in the picture of Smith stumbling when

she'd mentioned the police and dismissed everything involving Henri after that point. The important part of the tale was told.

'And how did he react?'

'Honestly, I think he was scared. He backed off straight away. People like that are so used to putting others down to make themselves feel good they don't know how to react when they fight back.'

If Henri had only given her a few minutes more to shut Smith down completely she mightn't feel a little short-changed now. He'd denied her closure at the last minute.

Gabrielle was all picture no sound as she placed the tray of cakes in the oven. Lola prayed she was imagining shooting down her own tormentors in similar fashion. It would do her good to let rip and tell them—tell anyone—how she felt.

'Okay, cupcakes are in the oven, cooling rack is ready—all we need now is the frosting.'

Lola yanked open the cupboard doors, searching for the crucial ingredients.

'Shoot! We're all out of icing sugar. I must've used the last of it on Bastien's cake.'

She'd gone through a truckload of supplies since starting at the hospital, self-medicating after run-ins with infuriating registrars and difficult patients.

'I can go get some.'

Gabrielle yanked off her apron and ran out through the kitchen door before Lola could stop her.

'Uncle Henri, I'm just popping across the road to get some icing sugar. I won't be long.'

Lola wasn't sure which of the two adults was more horrified by that suggestion—although probably for different reasons.

'I'll go. I don't want you crossing that busy road on your own.'

Henri sprang up from the sofa with the same eagerness as Gabrielle. People were so desperate to get away from Lola she was in danger of developing a complex.

Gabrielle rolled her eyes. 'I know how to cross a road. I'm not *five*.'

'All she has to do is cross at the lights.'

As much as Lola didn't want to be left with Henri and be forced to have the talk she'd steered well away from for days, it was important Gabrielle was afforded some independence.

'Make sure you do,' he told his niece as he bowed to the pressure and handed her some money from his wallet. 'I'll be back in a minute.'

Gabrielle almost skipped out of the apartment, drunk on her new freedom. It was amazing how much a small concession had changed her mood. Step by step they were gradually building her up. The ultimate goal was to give her enough confidence and self-belief that her detractors' cruel words would no longer hold any power over her.

'Be careful!' Henri and Lola shouted at the same time to the slamming door.

They exchanged the awkward smiles of two people unwittingly set up on a date. Except for the fact that it was her own fault they were out of supplies, Lola might have questioned Gabrielle's motives for volunteering.

'She's growing up fast.' Henri sighed staring longingly at the back of the door.

'Yes—and you have to let her. Trust me. I've been there with my brothers. I can only advise you from my point of view, as someone who's been there and is still wearing the "Wrapped in Cotton Wool" T-shirt, but you can't stop her from living her life and she'll only resent it if you do.'

Henri scrubbed his hands through his hair, mussing the once sleek locks as if he was battling the idea of letting go.

'Something's been bothering me since, you know… Well, a lot's bothering me…'

'Spit it out, Henri. It's not like you to be lost for words.'

They might as well get this sorted now, so she could stop swerving out of his path at work and get on with her job. He'd kissed her—he regretted it. There was little to get het up about as far as she could see. She kept telling herself that every time she replayed the moment in slow motion.

'What happened to you…it's not what Gabrielle's going through, is it? I mean, I've tried to convince myself that if things were that bad you'd tell me. I'd kill anyone who laid a finger on her.'

He was so agitated Lola knew she would have to put him out of his misery before he decided to lock Gabrielle in a tower somewhere for the rest of her life.

'No. Nothing like that. She has a low self-esteem issue—but, hey, who hasn't? Present company excluded…' Lola attempted to bring some levity back into the situation before he tried to shake the information out of her.

He closed his eyes and let a hissing breath out through clenched teeth. 'Thank goodness. I couldn't imagine having to go through that. *Je suis désolé*. That sounds so insensitive. How are you…after everything?'

Lola tried not to feel like an afterthought. It was perfectly normal that his main concern should be for his niece.

'Honestly? I was ticked off at you for taking over the care of my patient. It doesn't reflect well on me as a doctor if I'm not trusted to even suture a minor cut on my own.'

'That's not what it was about and you know it, Lola. The guy had his hands all over you—not to mention whatever went on between you in the past. I acted the way I would for any of my friends and family and I made sure that you were out of danger, first and foremost.'

Deep down, she knew that, but ingrained paranoia

wouldn't let her believe that a man would get involved in her problems for purely altruistic motives. Except for her brothers, who wanted to keep her under lock and key, and she certainly didn't want another prison guard keeping tabs on her every move.

'I appreciate your concern, but for the record it's not necessary. I'm not going to get anywhere if I don't learn to stand on my own two feet.'

'Message received and understood. Now can we talk about the *other* elephant in the room?'

Now would be a good time for Gabrielle to return, so Lola could slink back to her safe place.

'I really don't think that's necessary.'

'No? Then why have you been avoiding me? All I wanted to do was apologise to you. It should never have happened. I just…I don't know… You were upset… I wanted to comfort you. That's how it started, at least. But I had no right to kiss you. I don't blame you for hating me for betraying your trust like that.'

He loosened his tie and opened the top button of his shirt as he confronted his actions. And hers.

'I don't hate you. For that you would've had to have done something wrong.'

Her cheeks burned as she made her admission. She'd enjoyed having his lips on hers, but he shouldn't read any more into it than the fact that she'd gone too long without physical contact.

He tilted his head to one side and gave her his confused puppy face. He was really going to make her spell it out.

'I didn't entirely *hate* the kiss. Okay?'

Heat enveloped her whole body. With any luck it would burn a hole in the floor for her to disappear into.

'Now that we've got that out of the way I…er…should go check on the cupcakes.'

And stick her head in the oven while she was at it.

'Pardon?'

For an intelligent, worldly man, he was very slow on the uptake. The mystery of his single status was solved if he took *this* long to realise when a woman was telling him she liked him.

'For goodness' sake. Henri.' Lola threw her hands up in the air and walked towards the kitchen.

Gabrielle would be back soon, so there was no point getting into this now. He was off the hook, and she'd made a prat of herself for nothing.

She donned her oven gloves and waited for cake therapy to take effect. Unfortunately Henri was standing between her and her salvation.

'How can I believe you wanted that kiss when you were so tense in my arms?'

'I was confused. It had been a stressful day, if you remember? Now, I'm not going to stroke your ego any more. If you'll move out of the way, I'll get back to what tonight's supposed to be about. Gabrielle and cake. Nothing more.'

He folded his arms and leaned against the worktop, clearly with no intention of moving out of her way.

'If that was you enjoying yourself, I'm starting to feel a little hard done by.'

'Too bad.'

Her heart did that same stupid jig when he'd made a move on her the last time—and he wasn't even touching her. Yet.

'Why don't we try it again? Only this time going into it with our eyes open. Figuratively speaking, of course.'

He pushed himself off the counter and took a step towards her. Lola bit back a squeal but stayed firm, slowly nodding her response. What harm could one more kiss do now? It wasn't as if they were going to embark on some red-hot affair and blur that line between work and play even more. This was about satisfying her curiosity and salving Henri's bruised male ego. A Frenchman believing he'd failed as a Lothario must be devastating.

He came at her with such force he nearly knocked her off her feet. She clung to him, her stupid oven gloves around his neck, struggling to stay upright as he claimed her mouth. This time his lips were hard and demanding, yet every bit as passionate. She melted into him like chocolate in the sun and forgot all about her golden rule about keeping work and play strictly separate. And he was definitely prettier than her.

Perhaps it was that comforting smell wafting from the oven, or the knowledge that she definitely wanted this, but kissing Lola tasted even sweeter than he remembered. She was moulded to him, every one of her curves pressed against him, and preventing all logic from getting to his brain.

It didn't matter that they were colleagues or that he couldn't commit to someone with more baggage than he when she was teasing his tongue with the tip of hers.

He let his hands slide over the curve of her hips and down to the swell of her buttocks. She moaned when he pulled her flush against him, and there was a real danger that there was more than the cupcakes getting burned here. There was a fire blazing inside him for Lola, and only one possible way of extinguishing it. A kiss was one thing. Taking it any further would complicate all aspects of his life.

With great reluctance he loosened his hold and gave her one last soft kiss. 'This is probably a really bad idea.'

'Yeah. Probably.'

She looked up at him with desire-darkened eyes which didn't reflect what she was saying. Her lips were parted, swollen from his tending and inviting more.

In the scheme of things, he didn't see how much damage one last kiss could do. He moved in again, fastening his mouth on hers and warming himself in the last of their passion before the cold wind of reality blew out the flames.

A cacophony of noise rang out around them as if they'd triggered a *What the hell are you thinking?* alarm. The ear-splitting beep from the oven timer had gone off at the same time as Gabrielle sounded the doorbell.

Henri sprang away from Lola like a horny teenager busted by his parents while making out with his girl.

'I'll get that.'

'I'll get these.'

Lola scuttled away to rescue her and Gabrielle's cooking efforts, letting her hair fall across her face so Henri couldn't read her properly. She was as bad as his introverted niece at times—so careful not to let him know how she was feeling at any given moment.

Was he really so scary that no one could relax around him and say what was on their mind?

The irritating drone of the bell carried on until he was forced to leave Lola and their moment in the kitchen to answer the door.

'I thought you'd got lost,' he said, opening the door once he'd straightened his clothes.

'I was only gone for, like, five minutes.'

Another roll of exasperated teenager eyes and Gabrielle took herself and her purchases to the hub of the apartment. Everything important tonight was going on in that kitchen.

Henri checked his watch and confirmed the time. Five minutes was all it had taken for his world to be completely turned upside down. With anyone else a kiss wouldn't be such a big deal. Hell, he'd done more than that with women he barely knew. It held so much more meaning with someone like Lola, who was slowly easing her way into his life.

He couldn't promise her anything when he had so many

commitments elsewhere. Yet he didn't think he was capable of resuming a strictly professional relationship now that he'd had a sample of what he might be missing. That side of her he'd seen in Angelique's class hadn't been a fluke. Behind that shy interior there was most definitely a passionate showgirl waiting to be coaxed into the spotlight. Lord help him, but *he* wanted to be the one to help her shine.

Henri flopped down onto the sofa, content to leave Lola and Gabrielle to bond over their baking whilst he was left alone with his thoughts. It didn't happen very often without someone requiring his assistance.

He'd only just relaxed back into the seat when Gabrielle screamed, and he was back on his feet and running in no time.

'What is it? What's happened?' His doctor instinct kicked in and he burst through the door to assess the scene and see what he could do to help.

He slid on the sticky red trail splattered across the kitchen floor. The carnage was worse than he'd feared. Gabrielle shrieked again as Lola attacked.

'What the hell…?'

'We got a bit carried away…sorry.' Lola grinned at him, chocolate frosting dripping from her chin, her hair white and caked in flour.

'So I see.' Henri surveyed the kitchen, in the aftermath of an apparent food fight.

'She started it!' Gabrielle squealed from behind a fetching buttercream beard.

'Well, I'm finishing it. Your mother will have both our lives if you go home like that.' It was true, Angelique would not be happy, but it was good to see his niece having fun for a change.

'Spoilsport!'

He turned at Lola's insult—only to meet a blob of chocolate cream flying through the air at him. Gabrielle was doubled over laughing as he scraped away the brown dollop and flung it back at Lola.

'Oh, you think that's *funny*, do you?'

He helped himself to the bowl of ready-made icing and prowled towards the giggling teenager. She ducked behind Lola, unable to hide the wide smile spreading across her face. Henri couldn't remember the last time they'd laughed together like this, and it was all down to Lola.

'Run, Gabrielle! Save yourself! I'll cover you.'

Lola blocked him at every turn, protecting her charge until she could make a run for it. Gabrielle sprinted out through the door and down the hall, and the sound of the lock turning on the bathroom door told them she'd made a successful escape.

'Very brave, Miss Lola. Unfortunately you've put yourself directly in the line of fire…'

He scooped out a handful of sweet goo and spread it over her face. Not to be outmanoeuvred, Lola returned the favour, until they stood facing each other as painted warriors.

'You don't scare me,' she said through short breaths.

'No?' He watched her chest rise and fall more quickly with every step closer he took.

'Maybe a little.'

'You *are* very pale.'

He caught a blob of icing on her lip with his finger, but before he could wipe it away Lola caught it with her tongue. Every part of Henri stood to attention when she drew his fingertip into her mouth and sucked it clean. Her mischievous grin said she knew exactly what she was doing to him—and where.

'Is it safe to come out yet?' Gabrielle yelled from the bathroom, and the guilty pair separated to a respectable distance.

'Yes, we've called a truce. Now get your butt out here and help clean up.'

Henri didn't want her to catch them in the act. There was no way of knowing how she'd react to her uncle and her friend getting it on. Even if she didn't mind, there was no point in getting her hopes up that this was some epic love affair when he didn't know what he was doing. If he started something with Lola and regretted it later there was every chance he could break more than one heart along the way.

A clean version of his previously flour-dusted niece appeared, shaking her head when she saw the iced faces before her.

'You two are such dorks.'

'You love us, really. Come here and give us a big hug.'

Henri and Lola flanked Gabrielle and moved in for a two-pronged attack, wrapping her in a group hug to smoosh their faces against hers.

Gabrielle's laugh reached deep inside to touch Henri's heart. Moments like this were few and far between when he and Angelique were so caught up in work. He made a mental note to set more time aside in future to have fun with the kids and remember that there was more to being a replacement father than rules and school pickups.

'Okay, guys, I think playtime is over. We'd better get this mess cleared up before Jules gets home or we're all in trouble.'

Lola was the first one to break the huddle and Henri reluctantly followed her instructions. In that happy kitchen all the stresses in his life had ebbed away and he'd acted without worrying about the consequences. Now he'd have to return to being the responsible adult who so many counted on.

After cleaning up, they sampled the fruits of the girls'

labour until all three of them were in danger of going into a sugar coma.

'You can take the rest back for your mum and Bastien.' Lola boxed up the remainder of the cupcakes for Gabrielle, effectively ending the evening.

'Thanks for tonight.' Gabrielle reached up to give Lola a peck on the cheek as they left.

'Yes, thanks for everything,' Henri said as he, too, planted a kiss on her cheek.

If Gabrielle hadn't been there he might well have asked Lola for more. More than either of them were ready for. Perhaps this was one time when his responsibility to his family had saved him from making a huge mistake.

CHAPTER SIX

'Okay, Mr Rutherford, the X-ray confirms there is a fracture in your shoulder, but the bone hasn't moved so we don't have to operate.'

Lola's burly rugby-playing patient was visibly relieved at the news. She'd warned him they might have to pin the shoulder, since the fracture was so close to the joint, but he was safe for now.

'Thanks, Doctor.' The shaven-headed, mud-splattered muscleman might look intimidating on the outside, but he'd been a model patient since his admittance and very respectful to Lola as she'd assessed him.

She'd have to stop being so judgemental about people's appearances when she knew how it felt to be on the receiving end of such shallow prejudice. If she hadn't spent so much time with Henri she'd still think of him as an arrogant Frenchman who cared for nothing except himself. It was their secret that he was a loving, caring family man whose kisses were more addictive than a tray of chocolate-chip cookies.

Lola got her mind back on the job and went to work fitting a sling around her patient to keep his arm immobile. There was still some residual panic at being on her own with a member of the opposite sex who could clearly overpower her if he chose to. Perhaps that fear would never en-

tirely leave. But she was working through it. She also had
the safety net of knowing one shout would bring Henri to
her aid, and that notion of support without being suffo-
cated was a novelty for her.

With each patient she treated successfully Lola was
growing stronger. It was a shame Henri hadn't been there
to witness her progression. She hadn't seen him since that
night in her apartment, and old insecurities made her question his absence.

It was unfair of him to kiss her and leave her in limbo
about what happened next. For her, responding to their
attraction had added a new dimension to her life. Since
leaving high school her main goal had been survival. So
far she'd put herself through medical school, moved out
of home, and now was starting a new career. There was
some semblance of a normal human being emerging, but
there was one aspect of adult life she'd thus far avoided.

Her track record with men was short and traumatic,
and not something she'd seen the need to explore further.
Until Henri had kissed her.

That desire, the tenderness in his every touch, was
something she hadn't experienced in a long time, and she
hadn't realised how much she was missing it. If there was
a way to capture that passion and romance without handing over control of her life she might be tempted into *more*
French kissing.

Now that she was inextricably linked to his family she
didn't think Henri would intentionally hurt her and face
the wrath of his sister and niece. Nor did she expect him
to want to enter into any sort of long-lasting affair when
he had so many other commitments. That suited her fine.
She was only here for another month, and a fun, flirty
fling might be just the thing to help her finally move on.

All she had to do now was get Henri on board before
he had time to regret ever laying his lips on her.

'Hello, sis.' The sound of her brother's voice automatically shut out all thoughts of romance.

'Jake? What's wrong?'

Lola did a quick assessment to see what injury he might have been admitted with, but since he was standing upright, with no visible signs of blood, it didn't appear too serious.

'Nothing. I thought I'd pop in and see how you were since we haven't heard from you in days. Kyle and Matt are busy at the garage, otherwise they would've come, too.'

He'd find himself in Admissions very shortly, with the mobile phone he was waving in her face shoved somewhere the sun didn't shine for turning up here unannounced.

'You can't "pop in" whenever you feel like it, Jake. This is a busy hospital and you'll get me in trouble. Please feel free to pass that on to the other two.' She hooked her arm through Jake's and escorted him out of the department and back towards Reception.

Naturally this was the very moment she should cross paths with the elusive Henri.

He did a double-take as he passed them in the corridor. 'Is everything all right here?'

It was on the tip of Lola's tongue to explain the situation, but then she'd run the risk of another lecture about getting her priorities right. It wouldn't go down well for him to find out she was dealing with family matters when there was a queue of patients waiting to see a doctor.

'All under control, thank you, Dr Benoit.' She tugged at Jake's arm, determined to ditch him as soon as possible.

'The level of personal attention you give your patients is very admirable, but I think you might be needed back on duty.'

Henri was letting her know this was another black mark against her—and she'd been doing so well.

'Of course. I'm heading straight back after this.'

As soon as her toe had connected with her brother's rear end.

Far from impressing Henri with her feminine wiles, all she'd succeeded in was annoying him again. She dug her nails into Jake's arm.

'Ouch! What was *that* for?' he grumbled when Henri was out of earshot.

'I *told* you I'd get in trouble.'

Now she had *two* areas to work on with Henri before she'd get anywhere.

'Who's that? A foreign exchange student? Can I put in a request for a hot blonde next time?'

Jake wasn't being serious. Lola knew he didn't have a preference when it came to a woman's hair colour. Blondes, brunettes, redheads—they'd all claimed space in his bed over the years. He was an equal opportunities Casanova, who'd probably think all his Christmases had come at once if he had any inkling there was a burlesque-dancing Frenchwoman in town.

'That was my boss—so I *really* need to get back before I get the sack.'

She led him to the exit and all but pushed him out through the door. He really wasn't making this independence thing easy for her.

'Well, boss or not, he has no right to speak to you that way. Do you want me to have a word?'

Jake rolled up his sleeves, ready for his own brand of talking. If it hadn't been for everything Lola had endured, and the reasons behind her brothers' fierce need to protect her, she might have found it sweet.

As it was, their concern was holding her back from enjoying her new life to the full. 'No, Jake. I'm twenty-five years old. I can fight my own battles when I need to.' She kissed him on the cheek. 'I'll make sure to check in with everybody when I get some free time.'

'Okay…'

If he was unhappy with that arrangement he was smart enough not to say it. Small steps.

Lola waved him off, even though her legs were itching to run. She had to catch up on her workload and somehow get back into Henri's good books before they completely lost momentum.

Jealousy was an alien concept to Henri but there it was, snaking through his veins and poisoning his whole system until he couldn't breathe. He shouldn't have looked back. Then he wouldn't have seen her kiss the handsome stranger on the cheek, sending a dagger straight to his heart. Only a matter of days ago she'd had her arms around *his* neck, her lips pressed to his and her body language telling him she wanted more.

He turned away in disgust and kept walking, every stride longer and quicker as he fought to leave the scene. This was *his* fault. He'd been too slow to acknowledge how much Lola meant to him and now someone else had swept in and turned her head.

Why would a beautiful, intelligent woman such as Lola sit around waiting for a few scraps of encouragement from a guy too wrapped up in his own world to appreciate her? Only an idiot would let her slip through his fingers, and since he'd never followed up on that kiss in her apartment Henri *was* that idiot.

All he'd had to do was take Gabrielle home and go back to Lola. Hell, he could even have phoned her and arranged a proper date—anything to show her he was interested. Instead he'd walked away and left her vulnerable to every predatory male who happened by. With her history she deserved better than that.

Lola had shared something painful with him when she'd told him about her past, and it gave them a deeper connection than he imagined she had with this fly-by-night Lothario. It was possible Henri had been overly cautious about getting involved with her, partly because of everything she'd gone through, but she needed someone who understood and respected her. Someone who would never hurt her.

If she was ready to move on, Henri intended to be that someone. He only prayed it wasn't too late.

With his thoughts occupied elsewhere, he completed his rounds on autopilot. He said and did all the right things, giving credit to the staff where it was due and pointing out gaps in their knowledge that needed improvement. All the time he was trying to come to terms with the carnage a couple of kisses and a dinosaur cake had caused.

Now questions were rumbling in his head about how he actually *felt* about Lola and what, if anything, he could do about it. In the past his relationships with the opposite sex had been separated into two categories—friends and lovers, with never the twain to meet. It kept things simple when everyone knew where they stood, with no expectations placed on either party.

Lola was different. Everything he wanted wrapped up in one sexy package. It was a pity he'd woken up to that fact too late.

He dropped his stack of patient files with a thud, earning a scowl from the senior nurse he'd disturbed at the other end of the desk. Whoever this new guy was on the scene, he couldn't have got much of a lead over Henri. This was the first time he'd seen him with Lola, and she'd kissed him on the cheek—not the mouth. Perhaps it was early days for the couple and Henri still had time to make his move.

Then what? He couldn't offer her any more than an affair, and that mightn't sound as appealing to Lola as it did to him.

Right now he couldn't see beyond his own desires, which consisted of being with Lola and getting this other potential suitor out of the equation. It would require some cunning on his part, and the assistance of two irresistible children to make it happen.

It was late afternoon when Lola had to track Henri down for help with a case involving an elderly man with breathing difficulties. Despite the patient's insistence that he felt well enough to go home after Lola had administered some oxygen, she thought the wheezing in his chest was still cause for concern. A chest X-ray had shown signs of infection, but she wanted confirmation from a senior that it was necessary to admit him overnight for further treatment.

'Good call,' Henri said, stringing his stethoscope back around his neck after sounding the patient's chest and taking a look at the X-rays. 'We'll put in a request to get him moved to a ward, and start intravenous antibiotics as soon as possible to get the infection cleared.'

Although he'd concurred with her diagnosis, Lola wished she'd been confident enough to give the final say on the admission. 'I know I'm second-guessing myself, but I want to be certain I'm making the right judgement call.'

'I don't think we're ever really one hundred per cent sure on any case—we're not invincible—and you're right to check rather than take a gamble. But at some point you're going to have to show confidence in yourself and your diagnosis. How else will a patient feel safe in your hands?'

Once again Henri prompted her to consider how she could improve her standing here. Without the eyes of the other first-year doctors watching the exchange Lola didn't have the same inclination to want to cry. She took the comments in the manner with which they were made—

as advice from a superior who wanted her to be the best doctor she could be.

At the minute it was the more personal aspect of her relationship with Henri which was bothering her. One word was probably all it would take for her to fall back into his arms. A braver soul would have asked him outright what those kisses had meant—if anything. Had it been it a heat-of-the-moment reaction to the smell of home baking, or did he genuinely have feelings for her?

She should be bold and ask him outright if she meant to reinvent herself as the sort of woman who could embark on a fling without a second thought.

'I'm working on it.'

She hovered by the desk, waiting for some acknowledgement that their friendship had progressed to something more. But instead of a smile, a blush, or an action replay, Henri simply buried his head back in his paperwork. She took a seat in the empty chair next to him, close enough that she could read the handwriting on his reports. Flirting was a distant memory for her, but she was pretty sure it shouldn't result in the other person pedalling away on a swivel chair.

'Is there something else I can help you with?'

He was flicking through his personal diary at a rate of knots, oblivious to her attempt to rekindle the romance between them. Lola's bravado left her instantly.

Someone like Henri wouldn't have lost any sleep over a couple of snatched kisses with an easily impressed new intern. It hadn't been as much of a life-changing moment for him or an affirmation of his sexuality as it had for her. The idea that a sexy French doctor found her attractive in the first place should have been enough of a confidence boost without the expectation of more.

'I can see you're busy. It can wait.'

Next time she'd wait for the other party to make a move

and save herself from the crippling embarrassment of rejection or, worse still, this apparent apathy towards her.

She slid her chair away, prepared to freewheel the whole way down the corridor before she would stand up and walk away under a cloud of shame.

'Don't go.'

Henri shot his hand out to stop her, catching her above the knee, his fingers branding the skin. She wouldn't let herself get carried away with the idea that this was in any way a demonstration of his devotion—more likely he wanted to discuss her patient's aftercare.

'Did I forget something?'

She'd already made arrangements for the patient's transfer onto a main ward and informed him and his wife of their plans. There was nothing else she could have done as far as she was aware.

'No. You were great. Nothing to worry about on that score.'

He was distracted again, pulling up the rota on the computer screen and cross-referencing it with his planner. This was doing nothing to put Lola's mind at ease.

She sat with her hands in her lap, doing her best not to rub at the spot where his hand had rested and give him any indication that she was affected by his touch.

'Is there something I *should* be concerned about?'

Henri slammed his diary shut and swivelled around to face her. 'I might need your help with something. Angelique has been offered a fantastic opportunity to take part in a burlesque event in Paris as a last-minute replacement for another dancer. The childminder is away on holiday, and I'm supposed to be at a conference this weekend. I wouldn't ask, but—'

'You want me to babysit?' Lola's once soaring heart plummeted into her shoes.

He was only keeping her sweet so there was someone

on call to share the substitute parenting load. If she didn't enjoy Gabrielle's company so much, or believe that this would help their bond, she would politely decline.

'No. Yes. Sort of. I thought perhaps the kids could come with me to the conference hotel. There's a pool and a tennis court. I'm sure there's plenty for them to do whilst I'm in lectures.'

Henri fidgeted with the clasp on his diary, leaving the story half told. What was it he was expecting from her? She wasn't sure she was committed enough to go back and forth to God knew where in order to entertain his niece and nephew, regardless of their cuteness. For all he knew she could actually have a life outside of the hospital and his family.

'I'm sure a mini-break would do Gabrielle the world of good, but I'm not sure where I fit into your plans. I don't think I can commit myself to driving backwards and forwards every day to wherever it is you're staying.'

'I want you to come with us.'

'Pardon?'

Only the fact that he'd said 'us' and not 'me' stopped Lola from sliding off the chair and across the polished floor. This was moving faster than she'd anticipated even in her wildest, most erotic dreams.

'I know it's a lot to ask of you, but I don't want to let Angelique down when this means so much to her. The children are very fond of you, and I would prefer to leave them with you than to put them in some over-subscribed kids' club. I'll pay for everything—separate rooms, of course.'

There was no indication that he harboured any ulterior motive in getting her to the hotel other than babysitting. For 'separate rooms' she read, *Don't get any ideas*, and disappointment doused the flames of her ardour.

'I'd be glad to help out—and it will give Gabrielle and I more time to talk.'

Perhaps it wasn't such a bad thing that he wasn't planning a dirty weekend for the two of them. It took the pressure off having to reinvent herself as the sort of woman who jumped into bed with men on a whim.

Henri had picked up on that after one quick snog. There was no chance she would have carried that off if they'd ever made it to the bedroom. Her lights-off-and-duck-under-the-covers-before-anyone-can-see-me-naked approach to lovemaking wasn't conducive to the sizzling sex life the French were so famous for.

Getting involved with Henri would only serve as a reminder of how inadequate she still was as a woman. To date, her love life was a short and unsatisfactory tale for the few involved. The reality of sex had never quite lived up to the hype, and there was no reason to think even Henri could remedy that. Especially if the fault lay entirely at her feet and in her head.

There was little chance of her ever enjoying the physical side of a relationship when she wasn't comfortable with her body, never mind sharing it with someone else. This stint as his babysitter would put her firmly back into place as Henri's charge and nothing more.

The most she could hope to gain from the weekend was a chance to spend some alone time with Henri and the kids to help them bond, and at the very least she was getting an all-expenses-paid weekend away. All she had to lose was her heart. To the entire Benoit family.

With the conference being held in Donegal, crossing the border into Southern Ireland and changing their currency into euros had really given this work function more of a holiday vibe. Especially since he had a beautiful travelling companion seated next to him and a bouncy Bastien in the back seat.

'Uncle Henri says there's a pool and a park and *every-*

thing!' His nose was pressed against the window as they pulled up outside the majestic five-star hotel.

'It's amazing!' Lola leaned forward in the passenger seat as the castle-like building came into view.

It was perched high up on the hill, surrounded by a golf course and overlooking the sea. The isolation of the Donegal coast was the perfect destination for busy medical practitioners eager to escape the stresses and frantic pace of their profession. Only time would tell how suited it was to angsty teenagers and inquisitive six-year-olds. Not to mention the possibility of a romance.

'Glad you approve.'

Henri really wanted them both to relax over these next couple of days, so they could actually get to know each other. As much as was humanly possible whilst they were wrangling his niece and nephew.

He wasn't in the habit of employing family members to help him seduce women, but having Lola as their chaperon seemed a less salacious proposition than asking her to spend the weekend in a hotel alone with him. It mightn't be the most sophisticated or well thought out plan, but it was the best he could come up with at short notice—and better than sitting back and watching her being wooed by the competition.

All he wanted was the opportunity to explore this thing happening between them. There were so many sides to Lola she could never be simply another warm body for his bed when he needed it. But if he threw himself into a relationship with her there was the concern that it would detract his time and energy away from his other commitments. A couple of days and nights holed up here would tell him everything there was to know about the implications of getting involved with someone as kind and unselfish as Lola.

It hadn't been difficult to get Angelique on board since

she'd pitched the idea of working in Paris weeks ago. She had been offered a spot at her old haunt, that much was true, even if it wasn't as last-minute as he'd suggested to Lola. His sudden change of heart on the matter had raised Angelique's suspicions, but she'd jumped at the chance to have one last dance in Paris. After she'd phoned Lola to confirm she was voluntarily giving up her time to help out and not being held against her will, of course.

They were all exactly where they needed to be, and hopefully somewhere along the line he'd figure out the next stage of his plan.

Once they'd checked into the hotel, Henri insisted on carrying his and Lola's bags to their rooms. Angelique had packed the kids' things into rucksacks they were able to carry on their backs, much to Bastien's annoyance.

'This is so heavy I'm going to be too tired to play,' he said, collapsing onto the floor outside the bedroom door and showing his mother's flair for drama.

'Good. Maybe I'll get some peace.' Gabrielle stepped over him and let herself in with the key card.

'I hope you know what you're in for.'

Henri was talking to himself as much as his travelling companion. In the midst of his great idea he'd forgotten to factor in the time he'd spend refereeing between these two. He doubted the warring factions would call a truce long enough for any budding romance to fully bloom. They'd all be lucky if Lola didn't call it quits before the end of the night.

With the prospect of the bum-numbing talks he'd have to endure, and the sound of squabbling siblings, she was the one saving grace about this weekend.

'You mean this isn't all spa days and fine dining? How disappointing.'

Lola's eyes were bright with suppressed laughter, and Henri let go of the notion that he'd have to bribe his charges to behave. Unlike most single career women who crossed his path, Lola understood what these children meant to him and embraced everything that came with them. He didn't have to make apologies for who he was when he was with Lola.

'I know. I got you here under false pretences. Really you're in for forty-eight hours of tears, tantrums, and cries of "I'm bored!". And that's just me.'

'Well, you know where I am if you want me. I mean… just knock me up when you're ready. I mean…'

Lola slapped her forehead as she stumbled into one innuendo after another and Henri did his best not to burst out laughing. It gave him renewed hope to find he wasn't the only one preoccupied with thoughts of the bedroom.

'Lola Roberts, you have a one-track mind. I'm shocked. *Shocked*, I tell you.' He set her bag down at her feet and turned back to the room next door.

'Why is your face all red, Lola?' Bastien squinted up from his death throes on the floor.

Henri decided to save her any more blushes and lifted Bastien up by the rucksack so his legs and arms were dangling in the air.

'What I was trying to say was that I can take the kids as soon as you're ready.'

Lola had composed herself again, but Henri preferred her first offer. The one that didn't include a reference to anybody's offspring.

'I don't have any lectures to attend until the morning, so we could all go down together for dinner if you'd like?'

Although Henri had imagined a much more informal arrangement that would include drinks after the gruesome twosome had gone to bed.

Bastien's limbs windmilled in Henri's grip, wriggling like an insect picked up off the ground. 'I think I can walk now, Uncle Henri. Could you put me down, please?'

'Your uncle is an amazing doctor if he can cure broken legs with one hand.' Lola arched a cynical eyebrow at them both as the newly liberated Bastien bug ran into the room, laughing.

'I didn't get to be registrar for nothing,' Henri answered with a grin. 'Now, enough about my many, many, talents—tell me you'll join us for dinner?'

'Sure. I'll freshen up and meet you down in the restaurant in, say, an hour?'

They synchronised watches, then retreated to their separate rooms. Henri already knew the time he would spend with Lola would be the highlight of this entire weekend.

Henri's breath stuck in his throat as Lola walked into the restaurant. She'd swapped her casual travelling clothes for a floral baby doll dress that stopped just above her knees to show off her slim legs. Her hair was swept up into a messy bun, leaving her neck bare and begging for attention. Hers was a level of natural beauty that could never be achieved with an army of experts, and she had no idea how smitten half the room were with her as she wound through the tables.

Henri nearly spilled the jug of water over the table in his hurry to get to his feet and call her over. 'There's a seat here for you, Lola.'

'Hi, guys.'

She took the empty seat beside Henri and covered her knees with a napkin. Gabrielle cast a brief glance up from her games console, smiled, and resumed play. Bastien stopped playing the drums on the table with his spoon for long enough to say hello.

'You look beautiful.' With three little words Henri managed to turn Lola's cheeks the same pale pink as her dress.

'Thank you.'

She ducked away from the compliment when she should

have held her head high. No matter how hard he tried, Henri couldn't marry the two sides of her personality— that fearless siren he'd seen gyrating in Angelique's class, and the shy, insecure wallflower who hated any form of attention. Those low lifes must have really done a number on her if she couldn't see what he saw before him.

There was a great deal of whispering and elbowing going on from the opposite side of the table, and then Bastien threw his cutlery on the table and slumped into his chair. 'Uncle Henri, I don't feel very well.'

'Since when?' Not ten minutes ago Bastien had been using Henri's bed as a trampoline.

'Since now.' Bastien sighed, doing his best floppy rag-doll impression.

Henri left his seat and dropped to his knees in front of his nephew. He put a hand on his forehead. He wasn't running a temperature. 'You're not hot. Are you sore any-where?'

Bastien shook his head.

'Maybe he's homesick.' Gabrielle added her diagnosis and cuddled her brother tight.

Bastien nodded his head—much too eagerly for some-one supposedly ill. Gabrielle glared at him until he re-sumed his sad clown face. It was all highly suspicious.

'Is that right? And how do you propose we cure him, Dr Gabs?'

Henri didn't know what they were up to, but he was sure it had nothing to do with missing home. According to Angelique they'd been so excited to find out about their surprise getaway they'd barely slept last night.

'We could go back to the room and watch cartoons?'

He should have known they'd get bored sitting in a fancy restaurant when they were used to dinner on their laps with the TV on in the background. Henri tossed his napkin on the table. They didn't have to get the bill, since they hadn't had a chance even to order before the conspiring duo had concocted their own agenda for tonight.

'Cartoons it is, then. I'm sorry about dinner, Lola.'

'That's okay—the children are more important.'

Her resigned shrug and Lola's acceptance of his priorities should have warmed Henri, not left him cold. There was nothing he wanted more than to be with her, and he wished there was some way to convey that to her. So far this plan had backfired spectacularly. Rather than bringing he and Lola closer together, having the children here was pushing them further apart.

'No!'

Gabrielle's outburst made them all jump.

'I mean…that's not necessary. You two should stay and enjoy your dinner. I can take Bastien up to the room if you give me the key.'

'What about your dinner?' Sick or not, he didn't imagine that Bastien, away from the watchful eyes of his mother, would miss the chance to fill up on desserts without a good reason.

'We can order Room Service if Bastien starts to feel better.'

Gabrielle had it all worked out, and Henri wasn't sure what was behind it except for a chance to ditch the adults.

It was tempting to give in and finally have some quality time with Lola, but doubts still lingered. He glared at them, waiting for one of them to break and tell him what they were up to, but they simply batted their eyelashes and straightened their crooked halos.

Despite his reservations about leaving them to run riot through the hotel, he remembered Lola's words about giving Gabrielle more freedom. She was old enough to babysit her brother in a safe environment for an hour without getting into too much trouble.

He handed the key over with a word of warning. 'One dinner and one dessert only and I'll be up to check on you shortly.'

'Yes, Uncle Henri,' they chorused, and scampered out of the restaurant with the smiles of well-practised conmen.

Lola waited until they were out of sight before erupting into sweet laughter. 'They have you wrapped around their little fingers!'

'Ever get the feeling you've been had?'

Henri moved across to take the seat Gabrielle had vacated, so they were sitting face on, instead of side by side, with him trying to sneak a peek at her when he thought she wasn't looking.

'Definitely—but they're good kids. I don't think we need to worry about them ending up on the wrong side of the law just yet.'

'Perhaps not, but there's every possibility they'll have drowned in ice cream by the time I go up.' Unsupervised Room Service was probably an accident waiting to happen, but he was doing his best to adopt this new laid-back approach to substitute parenting Lola had advocated.

With the table now a child-free zone, Henri ordered some wine to accompany their preferences from the menu. It was beginning to feel more like a date—exactly what he'd hoped for—and yet a little Dutch courage wouldn't go amiss. There was every chance Lola could reject his idea of a fling, in which case he'd screwed *everything* up.

They waited in silence as the wine was poured, and Henri could see Lola's hands tremble as she lifted the glass to her lips. There would be no need for nerves if she saw him as only a friend.

He sawed into his steak with renewed gusto, fortifying

himself for the moment when he'd have to disclose his real motive for bringing her here.

Lola forced down every mouthful of dinner, even though her appetite had vanished along with the children. Without the accompaniment of minors she was simply a single woman being wined and dined by a handsome man. Something which her permanent state of spinsterhood didn't allow to happen very often. And it was being made especially difficult for her not to get carried away in the moment when neither one of them had any intention of going home at the end of the night.

She washed the growing anticipation down with a sip of wine, unwilling to get her hopes up that something could happen between them when Henri was here for work reasons, not her pleasure.

'Thanks for bringing me along this weekend. It's nice to get away for a few days.'

Although she'd had to bend the truth of her whereabouts to keep certain busybodies from interfering in proceedings. As long as her flatmate and her brothers didn't confer, she could come away from this without causing a scandal. There was no point in causing uproar over a potentially ruined reputation when any inappropriate behaviour was probably entirely in her head.

'It was for totally selfish reasons, I assure you. I didn't even ask if you had other plans.'

'Nope. I'm all yours.'

She took another gulp of wine after her clumsy attempt at flirting. There was no way she could bring herself to say what it was she wanted to come from their time together in case she'd got it completely wrong. She was trusting in Henri to read the signals and make the move. If he wanted to.

'What about the man you were with the other day? Are you sure *he* wasn't expecting your company tonight?'

Henri seemed to be toying with the food on his plate with the same enthusiasm Lola had for her own meal. When he gazed up at her, all that familiar bravado hidden beneath a furrowed brow, there was a genuine expression of worry that she'd rather be somewhere else.

Nothing could be further from the truth.

Lola blinked back at him mid-chew and swallowed the ball of anxiety in her throat. It was no doubt a difficult concept for Henri to grasp that she preferred some distance from her family. 'Jake? No, I told him I was busy. I'll catch up with him another time. And don't worry—he's been warned to stay away from the hospital in future.'

Henri placed his cutlery neatly in the centre of his plate with slow, deliberate movements. 'Whatever his name is, I hope he treats you right.'

'He's a pain in the backside, but he means well. It's just as well the other two are so busy with work at the minute or I'd have all *three* of them breathing down my neck.'

'All three of whom?' He was leaning across the table, eyebrows knitted together and staring at her as though she'd just landed on the planet.

'My brothers. Who did you *think* I meant?'

'I thought you'd traded me in for a triple threat.'

It took Lola a minute to comprehend the accusation of being a serial cheat. Once she'd stopped laughing she would put him right. Clearly her seduction technique needed work if he thought she was interested in anyone other than him. The thought of one romantic liaison brought her out in a cold sweat—any more than that would turn her into a complete basket case. She didn't know whether to be flattered or offended that he thought her capable of taking on three lovers.

I thought you'd traded me in...

Henri's words echoed in her head to remind her that he'd included himself in the list of her conquests and set her pulse fluttering once more. 'Are you saying you were jealous?'

'*Oui*. I don't want to think of you kissing anyone else the way you kissed me.'

Henri finally uttered the words guaranteed to make any woman swoon. But Lola's first instinct was to question his motives.

'Why not?'

This had to be about more than his ego being bruised or she'd inevitably end up getting hurt. It was important that he wanted *her* and not just a victory over some imagined foe. A one-sided love affair would never end well.

'I know we haven't talked about what happened between us, and that's entirely my fault. It was only seeing the possibility that I could lose you to someone else that made me face up to how much you mean to me.'

He reached across the table and took her hand, his touch reassuring her that this was frighteningly real and no longer a fantasy. However, she was realistic enough to understand that this couldn't be more than a fling. In a few weeks she'd be moving on to another department and Henri wouldn't give her another thought. If he wanted to be with her until then, it would be on her terms. At least that way she might be able to maintain some control over her emotions.

'I don't want anything serious, Henri. There's too much other stuff cluttering up my life to worry about being perfect girlfriend material. Got it?'

'I think I've got it. You want us to be lovers?'

The French accent was made to say that word. *Lovers*. It purred from his tongue, a deliciously exciting take on her blueprint for their future. The scandalous idea of using Henri only for sex was definitely a step forward in the adventures of New Lola. That way she'd get to have all the fun without any of the drama. *If* she was brave enough to agree to further involvement with a red-hot Frenchman with her limited experience. After all, Frenchmen were renowned for more than their egos and their cuisine.

'Yes.' She blurted it out before her insecurities caught up with her and convinced her that she wouldn't be enough for Henri—even as a lover. 'When my placement at the hospital is over, so are we. Both of us can move on with a clear conscience and our curiosity satisfied.'

That day in his office had given Lola a tantalising peek at what lay underneath his clothes. Now her body was on high alert at the promise of more. Goosebumps formed on the exposed skin of her arms and her nipples puckered against the thin fabric of her dress as arousal flooded through her, washing away any lingering doubts that she wanted this.

'*D'accord*. That's settled, then.' Henri tossed back the rest of his wine with the nonchalance of a Lothario who made indecent proposals every day of the week—when *she* could have done with a paper bag to breathe into.

Lola regretted not telling Jules about this weekend. She desperately needed her 'shut up and do it' brand of advice. Even though they were best friends, she hadn't shared with her any of the details about her involvement with the Benoits. Jules would undoubtedly have rejoiced at the idea of her roommate embarking on a torrid affair, but Lola wouldn't have been able to go to work every day imagining people sniggering behind her back. She'd had enough of that to last several lifetimes. But, paranoia aside, Lola was so far out of her comfort zone she needed one of Jules's motivational speeches to get her to the next level.

'The desserts look heavenly. Are you having one?'

Lola snatched the menu from the table even though her stomach was doing a double somersault. Another course would delay the moment when she would have to act on her side of this new verbal contract.

'No, I thought we could go back to the room. Unless *you* want one, of course?' Henri was antsy already, checking his watch and looking for the waiter.

Lola's once floaty chiffon dress was now clinging to the light perspiration on her skin. Her head was spinning as she fell into the fast-moving current of passion. She reached out and grabbed for her one lifeline before she was swept away with no chance of rescue. *My terms.*

'I don't want dessert, but I'm not sure I'm ready to simply jump into bed, either. I don't normally do this sort of thing. Could you give me a moment to get used to the idea first?'

Henri leaned across the table, forcing her to do the same so she could hear him. They were as close as they could be without touching, his breath caressing her lips in an almost kiss.

'I'm not an animal, *chérie*. As much as I want to be with you, I'm not going to drag you to bed before dinner even has a chance to settle. I just wanted to go and check on *les enfants*.'

He withdrew again, leaving Lola wanting to face-plant into the table. Who was the sex fiend now? All the while she'd been thinking Henri was desperate to ravage her and he only had the welfare of his sister's children on his mind. She'd have thought less of him in the long run if he'd abandoned their care in favour of his own selfish needs. Obviously the heat of the moment had warped her own sense of priority, since she'd completely forgotten she was there with anyone other than Henri.

'Of course we should make sure they're okay.'

Then she could go and hide under the duvet in her own room and spend the night revisiting her epic mistake in her head.

Once Henri had paid their bill they headed back to their rooms. The atmosphere during their journey in the elevator to the fourth floor was so charged Lola kept imagining he would make a move on her. *Hoping.* She couldn't remember the last time this level of anticipation hadn't had negative connotations. Medical school and work had all had her on tenterhooks in their own way, each forming that same weight of dread in her stomach as she waited for the sucker punch. This time, though, she was like a kid on Christmas Eve, impatient to get to the goodies.

Whilst she wasn't quite ready to consummate their new romance, there was no reason she couldn't have a little sample to tide her over. Her lips tingled with the memories of his, and she was tempted to take the initiative herself. If only it didn't seem so inappropriate now they were returning to their two mini-sized responsibilities on the other side of those metal doors.

The *ding* as they reached their floor signalled the end of their night, although Lola followed Henri to make sure the children were safe and sound.

Henri opened the door with the caution of a well-seasoned parent afraid to waken potentially sleeping little ones. He tiptoed inside and peered around the corner.

'Are they all right?' Lola whispered. Judging by Henri's muted reaction to the scene, they hadn't held any illegal raves in the hour they'd been left alone.

He backed out through the door again with his finger on his lips. 'They're asleep. Fully clothed and surrounded by dirty dishes, but asleep nonetheless.'

For a minute Lola could see his potential as a father. His loyalty to his sister was without question but there was more than a sense of him doing his duty where the children were concerned. From everything Lola had seen he was firm with them, and set boundaries where they were needed, but he was also very loving. He would make a great husband and father some day.

'I should get some sleep myself. Tomorrow is going to be a busy day.'

There was no formal itinerary planned, but she imagined a full twenty-four hours with Bastien would be an endurance test. She'd be sure to make full use of all the hotel amenities to fill the time for Bastien and Gabrielle in between Henri's appointments.

'Let me see you to your door—make sure you get home safely.' He closed the door and walked the two steps to her room.

'Well, goodnight. I'll see you in the morning.'

She went to unlock the door, but Henri settled his hand on top of hers to stop her.

'What? No goodnight kiss?'

His words warmed the back of her neck and turned her insides to liquid. One last smooch could be exactly what she needed to settle those bunched-up nerves and help her to sleep.

She turned slowly into his embrace, her breath hiccupping in her throat when he dipped his head to make good on his promise. Her eyes fluttered shut as he pressed his lips to hers, their gentle pressure soon building to the passionate exchange she'd been waiting for. Each time she was in his arms like this, being kissed in a way she'd only dreamed of, Henri chased away one of her bad memories to replace it with a happier, sexier one.

He cupped the curve of her backside and pulled her closer, fitting their bodies perfectly together. Lola heard herself moan and felt her hand slide from the door handle, all thoughts of leaving this corridor vanishing by the second. She was the filling in the sandwich between Henri's hard chest and the wooden door and she relished it. Pinned in place by his hands and lips, she'd never felt so wanted, so safe.

Lola all but slid to the floor when he let go of her.

'For the record, when we're both ready to take the next step you will have my *full* attention.'

His husky-voiced promise sent those goosebumps popping over Lola's skin once more and made the hairs on the back of her neck stand upright. If this was Henri when he was distracted, Lola wasn't sure she would survive him at full strength. Although she'd be happy to die trying.

On that thought, Henri took her hand and kissed it like a true gentleman. Only the wink as he left her gave away that devilish side she knew lurked within.

Lola sighed as she let herself into the bedroom, thoroughly dazed and now with absolutely no chance of a peaceful night's sleep.

CHAPTER SEVEN

HENRI WAS COUNTING down the time until he could join Lola and the children again. He'd talked about and listened to advances in emergency medicine enough for one day.

It wasn't that he thought he knew everything there was to know on the subject, but he could do with some light relief after talks on such topics as evaluating paediatric trauma and medical legal caveats. He always welcomed new techniques and important literature which would improve everyday patient care in the department, but he had a folder bulging with notes and leaflets still to digest before tomorrow's workshops.

At any other conference he would've stayed for the after-dinner drinks and the table quiz, where the competitive nature of those in the medical profession came to the fore, but he could think of better ways to wind down. He'd checked in with Lola on his mobile during the coffee breaks to find they'd all enjoyed a full sports programme while he'd spent the day sitting on his behind. Tennis, pitch and putt on the golf green and swimming were just a few of the activities Lola had listed when he'd asked what they were up to. Now, feeling guilty and sluggish, Henri was hoping for a quick dip in the pool before it closed for the night.

He hadn't expected to find anyone else splashing about

in the water. Especially not his niece and nephew, who really should have been getting ready for bed.

The urge to tell them off faded once he saw Lola in there with them. Engrossed in the sight of her frolicking without a care in the world, he paused to watch her from the changing-room door. Although she was wearing a conservative navy one-piece, it clung to all her curves and made Henri glad he'd chosen shorts over unforgiving Speedos. The clothes Lola usually wore, although unmistakably feminine, did not do her body justice. She was beautiful—inside and out.

This was as close to naked as he'd seen her and, coupled with his memory of last night's doorstep clinch, it was pure torture. As soon as this weekend was over and he could hand over parental responsibility to Angelique he was going all out to seduce her.

Lola had been half right when she'd accused him of wanting to drag her straight to bed. That was exactly what he'd wanted to do. But he'd used the kids as a barrier to protect her *and* himself from his libido. She deserved more than a quick release for his frustrations.

'Uncle Henri!'

Bastien's squeal echoed around the pool and immediately sent Lola ducking for cover. She dipped below the water so only her head was clearly visible and Henri was able to walk closer without fear of embarrassing himself.

'I thought you'd be safely tucked up in bed by now.' He climbed down the steps and launched into a front crawl towards the trio bobbing about in the far corner. The water was warm enough to soothe his tired limbs, but refreshing at the same time.

'We were having so much fun we must've lost track of time.'

Lola's smile vanished beneath the surface as Henri drew closer. The last thing he wanted to do was upset her and yet she didn't appear remotely pleased to see him. This wasn't the happy reunion he'd dreamt of during those never-ending lectures.

'Lola taught me how to swim. Wanna see?'

Bastien doggy-paddled over, a bright sight to behold in his orange swim cap, armbands and goggles. His face was a picture of pride as he puffed and splashed his way towards Henri.

'Well done, you—and well done, Lola.'

He caught Bastien up in his arms and planted a kiss on his head. It was a miracle she'd even got him near the water when bathtime was a battle of wills to get him to take his clothes off.

'Gabrielle's an amazing swimmer, too. I told her she should think about joining a local club.' Lola deflected his praise back to the teenager currently torpedoing the length of the pool.

'That's a good idea. If she's interested we can check it out at the local leisure centre.'

Henri had known Gabrielle could swim, but the speed with which she was moving was an eye-opener for him. This was the sort of skill he and Angelique should be encouraging, instead of leaving her to wallow in her teen angst. They hadn't worried too much about her lack of friends outside school, but a swimming club would be a great way for her to meet people her own age and get her out of the house on a regular basis.

Lola beamed as he promised to follow up on her suggestion. She was investing a lot of her time and effort into these two, and he was lucky to have found someone who didn't feel threatened by his role as their guardian. Part of the reason he didn't do long-term relationships was that most women invariably ended up resenting either him or the children for their drain on their time together.

Gabrielle made her way back in record time, breathless and smiling. 'Hey, Uncle Henri. How was your day?'

'Not nearly as much fun as yours, I suspect. I'm exhausted just watching you.'

Even Bastien was now starting to show signs of fatigue, simply floating on his back and staring at the ceiling.

'After the tennis and the golf I *am* starting to get tired. And thirsty.' Gabrielle hitched herself up onto the side of the pool and squeezed the water from her braid.

'Give me five minutes to get a couple of lengths in and we can all go up and have hot chocolate in the room before bed.'

Henri took over from his niece, slicing through the water, in a hurry to join the happy band of spectators before the end of the night. He pushed himself until his lungs were threatening to burst, gulping down a breath with each turn of his head as he made the return journey. Before he'd come to a full stop Lola was already out of the pool, chivvying the others towards the changing rooms.

'Lola—wait.' Henri hoisted himself up the steps, eager to catch her for a moment alone.

He was sure she'd heard him. Her steps had faltered for a second before she carried on running towards the door.

'Lola!' He made certain she heard him this time, his voice booming around the four walls.

She paused, her back still to him, forcing Henri to run a couple of steps ahead so he could face her.

'Didn't you hear me call you? I just wanted to say thanks for taking care of everything today.'

'No problem. I just want to get changed and then we can talk.'

She was acting very strangely, with her hands held up to her chin, her arms covering her chest. It wasn't as if he hadn't seen a woman in a swimsuit before, and, frankly, he hoped to see her in a lot less very soon.

'Is everything okay?' It was in his tactile nature to reach out to her, so he was taken aback to see her withdraw into herself so much she hunched over.

'Fine.'

Her teeth were chattering, even though the place was hotter than a sauna. Something was definitely amiss, but Henri didn't want to make her any more uncomfortable than she obviously was. He didn't know what had happened since last night to cause her to retreat again. Perhaps a day with two active children was more of a passion killer than he'd anticipated.

'I hope you're still going to join us for supper?' He wasn't averse to bribing Lola with chocolate to get a few more precious minutes with her.

'I will. As soon as I get changed.'

She was off again, the patter of her bare feet across the wet tiles marking her escape from whatever it was that had spooked her.

Since the others were in the ladies' changing room, Henri had time for a quick, uninterrupted shower.

Although he was always on hand to help out with the children, both he and Angelique had drawn the line at him moving in. He had even more respect for his sister coping so well without a partner since he was relying so heavily on Lola. Twenty-four hours with an inquisitive six-year-old had only reinforced how difficult it was for his sister to have some time on her own—or privacy, for that matter.

At least Henri wasn't shy about his body or it would have been awkward for him when Bastien had walked in on him this morning. *Oh, God!* If he'd bombarded Lola with the same questions about 'down there' it was no wonder she'd been anxious to cover up. And now he'd left her to wrangle Bastien on her own.

He jumped out of the shower and gave himself a quick towel-dry. His clothes stuck to the layer of moisture left on his skin, but it was a small price to pay to save Lola from having to explain to Bastien why she didn't have a winkie.

The three water nymphs were sitting, waiting for him on the couch outside the gym, all fully dressed and yawning. If Lola was traumatised by Bastien's quest to know everything about everything before he was seven, she hid it well by letting the nuisance in question curl up on her lap.

'I'll carry the Tasmanian Devil if you can manage the gym bags?' Henri handed his wet swimming stuff over and scooped Bastien up into his arms, not letting go until they were all safely inside the hotel room.

Bastien was still fast asleep when Henri put him to bed. He knew from experience that trying to get the child into his pyjamas now would be as easy as wrestling socks onto an octopus.

'Angelique will kill me if she finds out he's slept in his clothes two nights running.'

'I won't tell if you don't,' Lola whispered as she pulled the bedcovers around the sleeping babe. 'But it'll cost you that hot chocolate you promised me.'

Henri boiled the kettle and set three cups out, but Gabrielle shook her head. 'None for me, thanks. I'm cream-crackered. I just want to go to sleep. Why don't you and Lola take your hot chocolate into her room, so you can chat without worrying about keeping us awake?'

He applauded Gabrielle's attempt at matchmaking, even though it wasn't necessary. Lola's natural beauty and kind heart had captured his attention from the first moment she'd run into his A&E department.

'That's okay. I'm sure Henri wouldn't want to leave you alone. We can do it some other time.'

Lola was making more excuses not to be alone with him, but she'd underestimated the Benoit stubborn streak.

'You need some adult company. Now, stop talking and

let me get to sleep.' Gabrielle climbed into bed and ended the subject.

'There's no point in it going to waste.'

He held out a cup and Lola took it with a sigh, surrendering to the tag-team guilt trip. If nothing else was to come of being invited into her room, he was determined to discover what was behind the look of fear when he'd grabbed her arm earlier.

Lola's hands were shaking as she unlocked the door. It was little comfort knowing Henri's hands were occupied with steaming mugs of chocolate when his sheer presence in her room would be overwhelming. They'd agreed not to embark on anything out of her comfort zone until they'd handed Gabrielle and Bastien back to their mother, but things were progressing between them with each passing moment. Although there were some areas she clearly needed to work on...

Henri rounded on her as soon as they were inside and he'd set the cups aside. 'Do you want to tell me what that was all about down by the pool? Did Bastien do anything to upset you?'

'No. Not at all. It was just me being silly.'

She didn't want to take the blame for her hypersensitivity except the men who'd caused it in the first place. Not that there was a chance in hell of *that* happening. They were free to carry on with their lives, never looking back, while she couldn't seem to move on—no matter how hard she tried.

'It wasn't silly. I could see the terror in your eyes when I reached for you. Is it to do with what happened to you before?'

Henri kept his distance, as though he was afraid to touch her now, her skittishness having scared him off. The bullies had chalked up another victory.

She nodded, choking back her fear and determined to fight back. Henri deserved to know why she was still acting like a scared virgin when he'd done everything to make things easier for her. Perhaps if she actually gave that young, naïve Lola a voice she would regain some power over what had happened to her.

Henri stood silently, no longer cajoling and begging her to confide in him but waiting until she was ready.

Lola took a deep breath, in and out, exhaling all the anxiety that went with sharing the memory. 'I was a flat-chested, short-haired tomboy in my brothers' hand-me-down clothes. It was no wonder I was a target of ridicule. But that didn't mean I didn't have the same feelings as every other teenage girl, and I was flattered when the handsome rugby captain took a shine to me.'

She wanted to close her eyes and avoid that look of pity in Henri's eyes, but that would only make it easier for those hideous images to play back behind her lids.

'To cut a long story short—it was a prank. He got me to his house, his mates were there, and they held me down and stripped me to make sure I was a girl underneath the masculine clothes.'

Humiliation still burned all these years later. Her tears and screams had been drowned out in the cacophony of laughter and jeers.

'Bâtard!'

Lola's French was limited, but Henri's growl was enough to know he'd have dished out the same punishment as her brothers had.

'Needless to say, I have a few hang-ups about my body.'

'But you've had relationships since?'

It was so simple to someone so confident in themselves. Henri had probably never thought twice about anything that had happened to him in *his* teenage years.

Lola sat down on the edge of the bed, preparing herself

to carry on with her sorry story. 'In hindsight, I should
have gone to the police…had therapy. But I didn't have
anyone to turn to for advice except three bloodthirsty
brothers. I jumped from one disaster to another until I realised I'd be better off on my own.'

Her voice trailed off as she relived those moments of
defeat when boyfriends had grown tired of dealing with
her intimacy issues.

This time Henri came to her and knelt on the floor before her. 'They weren't worthy of you, Lola. Don't think
for one moment you are any less of a woman because of
what those scumbags did to you. You are beautiful. Never
be ashamed of who you are.'

She stroked his cheek and felt his jaw tense beneath her
palm. 'If only it was that easy.'

'Do you trust me, Lola?' He took her hands in his and
leaned in, capturing her in his intense gaze.

'Yes.'

She said it more confidently than she'd expected.
There'd been moments when she'd questioned his motives,
but she'd never been physically afraid of Henri.

He got to his feet, gently coaxing her off the bed to stand
with him. 'Will you let me undress you?'

'No.'

She attempted to sit down again. He'd overstepped the
mark. There was no way she was stripping here in front of
him when she was at her most vulnerable. Hell, she hadn't
even been able to let him see her in her swimsuit without
trying to hide her meagre assets.

He caught her by the wrist and pulled her up to face
him again. 'Do you trust me?'

'Yes, but which part about me being afraid don't you
get? I've spilled my guts about what happened to me and
all you can think about is getting me naked!'

She'd clearly underestimated who she was dealing with

if Henri was nothing more than just another sex-obsessed male, pretending to care so he could get her into bed. He might as well have ripped her heart out there and then.

'I only want to help you, Lola. This is why I'm asking for your permission to see you naked.'

The husky tone was back in his voice, making Lola's lady parts tingle despite her best efforts to remain immune to his request.

'Henri—' She didn't know where this was going, and that terrified her more than getting naked.

He let go of her hands, taking away her support. 'The next move is yours, *chérie*.'

'Only if you strip, too.' It didn't seem fair that she was the only one expected to be open to scrutiny. This wasn't a peep show.

'I will if you insist, but this isn't about me. How can we take the next step if you're not even comfortable in your own skin?'

Henri brushed his hand along her arm, electrifying all the little hairs he came into contact with and charging Lola with renewed sexual energy.

He was right. They were supposed to be embarking on a scorching, rip-each-other's-clothes-off sex-fest. Not a chaste game of peekaboo or a therapy session. She wanted this, she wanted Henri and she was simply going to have to be bold about it to make this work.

With trembling fingers she unzipped her dress. Unless he turned on the main light she'd remain in relative shadow anyway. She peeled down the top half and shimmied out of the rest until she remained in only her underwear and heels.

Henri moved behind her and bent down to whisper in her ear. 'All of your clothes.'

'I... I...' She shivered, frozen to the spot by his words.

'Would you like me to help you?'

She bit her lip and nodded, her quota of bravado all used up in one act.

Henri didn't give her time to change her mind. His hands were warm on her skin as he opened the clasp on her bra and let it fall to expose her breasts to the cool air. Lola automatically tried to cover herself again, but Henri laced his fingers through hers and pulled her hands away. Her shallow breaths grew louder in the darkened room as he whipped her panties down her legs. She was completely naked, in a hotel room, with her fully dressed work colleague.

'Open your eyes and look in the mirror.'

She hadn't realised how tightly shut they were until Henri made her face the dressing table mirror. It took everything for her not to look away again. She was so pale, so exposed against Henri's form it was hard to watch.

He traced his hand along the curve of her breast. '*Belle*. You are beautiful, Lola.'

She quivered as he kissed the back of her neck, brushing the sensitive spot which was apparently connected to her knees because they threatened to give way. The mirror played an erotic dream sequence before her eyes as Henri cupped her breasts in his large palms and rolled her nipples to hard points between his fingers. Another wave of arousal flashed through her, pooling at the apex of her thighs and completely disregarding any argument against this.

Henri carried on mapping her body with his slow caress, tracing over the indent at her waist and sweeping over her midriff. Lola felt her inner muscles contract as he dipped lower, anticipating his final destination. She held her breath and closed her eyes, waiting for him to claim her.

'Don't you want to watch?'

There was an agonising pause as he coaxed her back to face the couple reflected in the glass. When she saw the image of her pale, aroused body enveloped in the safe arms of a hunky male, Lola realised that was exactly what she wanted to do. She was ready to witness her own sexual awakening.

The pale figure in the mirror guided her lover's hand between her legs, throwing her head back in ecstasy as he pressed into her.

Henri slid a finger inside Lola, ignoring his own desires to see her needs put first. She might never have justice for what those bastards had done to her, but she deserved to live her life like any other woman. Without fear, and accepting of her own sexuality.

It was promising to find she was guiding him where she wanted him to be, taking control back. He pushed deeper, stroking her until her legs were trembling and her moans were driving him crazy.

'Do you want to lie on the bed?' he asked, whispering directly into her ear, causing another shudder to ripple through her limbs.

'Yes…'

Her breathy response did nothing to abate the tightening of his trousers.

She was slumped against him, her head resting against his shoulder and one hand reaching up to anchor around his neck. It was down to Henri to get her where he wanted her.

As easily as he'd carried Bastien, Henri scooped her up into his arms. Lola clung to him as he carried her to the bed, her hooded eyes watching him carefully but not expressing that fear he'd seen once too often. She trusted him, and he knew how much effort that must have taken.

He laid her down on the covers so her legs were dangling over the edge of the bed, opening her fully to him. Her chest rose and fell with every sharp breath she took and she chewed her bottom lip as he stood over her. It would take a little more to get her as relaxed as possible, but Henri was confident he was the one to help her.

With one hand either side of her head, he braced himself on the bed to kiss her without lowering his full weight on top of her. He gently drew her bottom lip into his mouth and slipped his tongue in to tangle with hers. It didn't take long before she went limp beneath him, lost in the kiss and almost persuading Henri to draft a new plan. His erection strained painfully between them, but he was willing to suffer some personal discomfort in order to give Lola what she needed.

'Is this okay?' He was trailing kisses down her throat and over her collarbone, but he wanted to make sure she was with him every step of the way.

'Mmm…hmm…' Lola sucked in a breath through her teeth as he latched on to her nipple and made no attempt to stop him. With every lick and suck of that hardening peak she writhed beneath him, her shyness forgotten as she rubbed her body against his.

With deft fingers, he plucked the other pink tip to a bullet point, and Lola arched off the bed in response. She grazed her soft mound into his ever-increasing hardness until Henri was forced to take a time out, waiting for the fireworks going off behind his eyelids to cease so he could focus back on Lola.

When the tremors subsided, Henri moved farther down her torso, pressing soft kisses against her chlorine and soap-scented skin until he was kneeling at her feet.

'If you tell me to stop, I will.'

He wanted her to know that even now, lying naked and exposed, she had the right to say no and have it heard. Although there was a catch in her breath, Lola nodded and gave him the green light.

Henri danced the tip of his tongue over her stomach, feeling her muscles tightening as he dared to go ever lower.

With his hands lifting her legs apart he buried himself between her thighs and lapped at her entrance. Lola's gasp spurred him on, and he plunged in to taste her arousal. Her legs were draped over his shoulders, her buttocks cupped in his hands, as he drove inside her and showed her how sex could be. Loving, enjoyable and totally freaking hot.

She was tugging his hair, scratching his neck with her nails, but never once did she ask him to stop. If the purring noises she was making were any indication, she had no intention of doing so. Henri circled that sweet bud, flicking and licking until Lola tensed around him. Even then he didn't stop. Through every contraction and release of her inner muscles he sought her out, unrelenting, until she almost bucked off the bed and cried out her release. Only when every last aftershock had left her body did Henri finally withdraw.

Lola lay panting on the bed, thoroughly ravished and gorgeous. Her mussed hair was a crooked golden halo around her head, her lips were swollen from his kisses and her legs were still parted and inviting. It would be so easy for Henri to take what he needed too, but that would make him no better than the other men she'd encountered. He wouldn't take advantage of her so callously.

Instead, he pulled the covers back on to the bed and helped her in.

'Thank you.'

From the glassy sheen of her tears, glinting in the darkness, he didn't think Lola was referring to him tucking her in. But sex wasn't something a beautiful woman should ever have to be grateful for. *Any* man should thank his lucky stars if he got close to Lola—he knew he did.

'My pleasure.' He kissed her on the forehead and received a lazy smile in return.

Something told Henri their idea of fun had just skipped to the next stage.

CHAPTER EIGHT

EVERY TIME LOLA cast her mind back to last night her body tingled with awareness and a smile crept across her face. She couldn't stop thinking about Henri and what he'd done to her—for her. More than the mind-blowing orgasm he'd given her, he'd literally made her face her fears.

Her tormentors' hold on her was gradually weakening under Henri's careful guidance. He was providing her with a special brand of therapy, ensuring she was at peace with her own body. It was easier to achieve when Henri had left her in no doubt about his attraction to her. In his company she was definitely all woman. There was no room for ambiguity any more.

'*Lo*-la!' Bastien cried out as the tennis ball whizzed by her head.

'Sorry!'

Despite her best attempts, the children hadn't had her full attention this morning. Since they'd all overslept, and with Henri having a lecture first thing, breakfast had been a rushed affair. It made her antsy. They hadn't even had a chance to talk in private, never mind embark on a follow-up to last night's events. Exhausted by her exertions, and released from her inner turmoil, she'd slept soundly, thanks to Henri.

At the age of twenty-five, Lola was looking forward

to her first adult relationship built on mutual trust and respect.

'I think you need a few more lessons.'

The mere sound of Henri's voice sent Lola into raptures. He caught the ball mid-flight in one hand and carried it over to her. The sun cast its favourable glow through his white shirt, highlighting the impressive muscles hidden under the 'sensible doctor' wear. Her body responded as if he'd stripped her naked again, her nipples beading under her T-shirt and that ache in her loins growing by the minute. There was every chance she would spontaneously combust if she was subjected to any more of his hotness without an outlet for her admiration.

'Are you offering?'

Her bravado was in direct correlation with her libido today. That moment she'd been avoiding couldn't come quickly enough now she'd had a taste of what Henri had to offer. His hands-on skills weren't limited to the workplace.

'Any time.'

The knowing wink he gave her was the stuff of erotic dreams—slightly ruined by Gabrielle's exaggerated cough and the reminder that there were children present.

'I thought you'd be caught up for at least another few hours?' She'd anticipated another day of outdoor pursuits to work through her Henri-less disappointment.

'I have all the notes I need, so I thought I'd ditch the workshop and get back to the fun stuff.'

Henri was addressing the kids, but Lola imagined he was talking to her. There was nothing she'd like better than to have more *fun* with him.

'Can we go home and see if Mum is back?' Bastien cast his racquet aside, clearly already taken with the notion.

'Is that what you want?' Henri asked, unable to hide the surprise and delight on his face. He checked his watch. 'I think Angelique's flight arrives in about two hours. If we're quick we could get to the airport in time to meet her. Everyone in favour of going home raise their hand.'

The unanimous decision was made as four hands shot up into the air. Although the hotel was fabulous, Lola couldn't wait to get back home and pick up with Henri where they'd left off.

'That's settled, then. As soon as we are ready we'll hit the road.'

Henri glanced over the heads of the bouncing children at Lola. The unspoken message was there that tonight was the night they'd finally leave all their baggage outside the bedroom door and focus on each other.

Lola had her bag packed in record time.

They collected Angelique from the airport and the children lit on her with fervent hugs and kisses. Lola didn't imagine they were parted very often, and it was sweet to see how much they'd missed each other. Even Henri wrapped his sister in a bear hug once Gabrielle and Bastien had let go of her.

The bond between the family wasn't unlike the one she shared with her brothers, and though Lola hated to admit it she was starting to miss them. So much had happened since her graduation, and there was no reason they couldn't share in the good times with her as well as the bad. If things went well between her and Henri she might even think about introducing him.

Once they were all delivered back to Angelique's house, with their assorted luggage, Angelique took Lola to one side.

'Thank you for everything. I haven't had a chance to say that, with all that's been going on, but I really appreciate your help. Between coming to the rescue with Bastien's cake, teaching Gabrielle how to bake and now babysitting, I don't know how I'll ever repay you.'

'It's no trouble at all—but I *was* going to ask about taking more of your classes.' The Benoits were certainly helping her to flourish, and Lola wanted to make the most of her newfound sensuality while the impetus was there.

'Say no more. The door's open for you any time. Anyone who can put a smile on my brother's face is worth their weight in gold.'

Angelique gave the same cheeky wink her sibling used to great effect. She was such a glamorous woman of the world...Lola imagined her tales of Parisian nights and Moulin Rouge-inspired experiences would put her own exploits with Henri to shame.

'Did you have a good time?' Lola didn't want to discuss her love life with her lover's sister. At least not until they'd fully established one.

'It was am-*a*-zing. I'm too old to make it as a chorus girl, but now I have that experience to cherish for ever. And, as glamorous and bohemian as that life is, I wouldn't want to give up what I have here. I'm a different person now.'

Angelique was beautiful now, in her mid-thirties, but she must have been a real stunner in her heyday. Given Gabrielle's age, her dancing career must have come to an abrupt end when they'd left France for Irish soil. Lola couldn't help but wonder if watching his sister's marriage crumble when she'd given up so much for love was part of the reason Henri wasn't interested in anything long term.

'Aren't we all?'

If these past weeks had proved anything, it was that people were evolving all the time—mostly for the better. The ones who stayed the same—well, they were losing out on all life had to offer.

'What's this? A girlie gossip?'

Henri slid his hands around Lola's waist, and the public display of affection in front of his sister was a milestone

as far as Lola could see. Angelique was too important to
him to let her in on their secret if it didn't mean anything
to him.

'Were your ears burning, little bro? I was just telling
Lola I can take it from here if you two have some...er...
catching up to do.'

Angelique and Henri exchanged cheesy grins while
Lola wanted to hide. This forthright French attitude to sex
took some getting used to.

'You know I love Gabs and Bastien...but, yeah, I'm of-
ficially handing them back to their mother. I have a life of
my own to get back to.'

He nuzzled Lola's neck, and it was all she could do not
to throw herself at him in the middle of the hallway.

'I *was* starting to wonder. Please, Lola, take him away
and spoil him. It's about time he had someone to take care
of him for a change.'

She shooed them out the door, not giving them time to
say goodbye to the kids. As well behaved as they were,
Lola was glad of some respite and fully intended to heed
Angelique's advice. Henri was so busy looking out for
other people, he put his own needs last. A matter Lola
would rectify as soon as possible.

The atmosphere inside the car was completely different
without the excitable children in the back. Now there were
only two super-charged adults, eager to get to their destination. It was a short drive across the city to Henri's bachelor pad—made even shorter as he put his foot down on
the accelerator. He barely abided by the speed limits as the
sexual tension inside the sports car fuelled their journey.

It was something of a relief when they pulled up outside the modern, detached villa that reflected his outward
personality to a T.

'Sorry, I should've asked if you wanted to go home
first.'

Henri pulled on the handbrake and gave her one last chance to change her mind. She didn't want to alter her path now, when this was the first step to her new beginning. Making love with Henri would change how she viewed herself and men for ever. It wasn't a view she would share, in case putting that much pressure on him ended in disaster.

'Jules isn't expecting me home until late. I don't need or want to be anywhere else.'

Lola's heart was in her mouth as she laid herself bare before him. One wrong move now and she could end up back at square one, crushed by the disappointment of her own inadequacy.

Henri was silent, the rustle as he removed his seat belt the only clue that he'd heard her request to stay. Lola unclipped hers too, making that commitment a firm reality. She reached for the door handle, deciding to take the initiative to go inside or else they'd end up sitting out here until it was time for her to go home. Now Henri knew exactly what he was taking on in this neurotic, damaged rookie doctor, Lola hoped he wasn't having second thoughts.

When the door didn't open, Henri reached over to do it for her. 'Child locks.'

They were chest to chest as he stretched across her, too close to ignore the magnetic force between them.

Their first hungry kiss was full of the pent-up lust and frustration built up over the last eighteen hours. Tongues vied for position and lips crashed together as the chemistry between them finally exploded.

The leather seat squeaked with every shift of their bodies, playing an unfortunate soundtrack against their passion.

'Shall. We. Take. This. Inside?' Henri asked between kisses.

Lola nodded, but it took several more smooches before

they finally broke apart. They abandoned their bags in the car in their haste to get indoors, lighting on each other as soon as the door closed behind them.

Lola had done enough talking, had her fair share of soul searching, and now all she wanted was to *feel*.

She plucked the buttons on Henri's shirt open, eagerly ripping off the wrapper from her present. His chest was smooth and taut and his firm abs rippled beneath her fingers. This was the body of a man—not some spotty teenager who thought he was God's gift, with free rein to treat people however badly he wanted.

They stripped each other on their way to the bedroom, leaving a trail of clothes and underwear in their wake.

With Henri naked beside her, this time Lola didn't shy away from his gaze. She stood firm as he swept his eyes over her body, regardless that she was quivering inside. Although she was still being judged, she knew it came from a place of appreciation. Henri definitely liked what he saw. And Lola temporarily forgot her own state of undress to marvel at his. His erection stood proud and unrelenting, a confirmation of his desire for her.

The moment her nerves started to creep back she clung to Henri, and every kiss and caress kept them at bay. He backed her onto the bed, his hard body covering the full length of hers. Once upon a time she would have found that intimidating, claustrophobic, knowing he could trap her beneath him with minimal effort. But this was Henri—not the ghost of boyfriends past. Everything he did was out of desire. Something she'd spent too long running from.

Already primed since last night, and with Henri's hardness pressing into her flesh, Lola knew she was ready. She lifted her hips to make full contact, rubbing against him so his shaft parted her entrance.

'Lola—' Henri groaned into her neck and a jolt shot south through her, turning her breath to a gasp.

Her body thrummed at the first touch of him, waiting for more. Another tilt of her pelvis drew him farther in, forced another ragged moan from his lips. He wanted this as much as she did, and she saw no point in their torturing each other any longer.

'I want you…' she breathed into his ear, knowing he couldn't hold out for ever.

A lifesaver, a guardian and a therapist he might be, but beneath it all he was primarily a man. She traced the outline of his ear with her tongue and sucked his lobe into her mouth.

His first blunt entry made her cry out—not through pain, but surprise. He filled her so completely it took a few moments for her to adjust to the new invasion.

'Are you okay?' Henri locked his arms out straight and levered himself off her.

Lola could feel him trembling from the restraint while he waited for reassurance that she was happy to continue.

'I'm fine.'

She took a few deep breaths, her inner muscles gradually easing to let him move freely again. He took his time at first, until she got used to taking all of him inside. The steady rhythm became familiar, relaxed her with every thrust, but the new Lola wanted more. She knew he was holding back—always thinking of her and what he thought she needed.

Lola ground against him, reached down to dig her nails into his buttocks and drive him on. Henri responded by withdrawing fully and then plunging straight back into her, their bodies slapping together with the force. With each new penetration Lola was drifting further from her body. The frequency and intensity increased in time with Henri's shallow breaths and Lola could hear herself moaning in response. She was climbing higher and higher. And then Henri pressed his thumb into her sex and the added pressure toppled her over the edge.

She clutched at his shoulders as she rode out her climax, releasing all her demons in one long cry. He chased his own satisfaction, pumping into her until he found it with a roar. When he'd given her everything he had, he fell onto the bed next to her.

They lay panting and smiling at each other, like two lovestruck teenagers experimenting with each other's bodies for the first time. In some ways she *was* that inexperienced young girl, finally discovering what all the fuss was about. It had probably always been this way for Henri, but she knew for sure that she wanted to discover if it would be as good between them every time.

There was only one way to find out, and as soon as they got their breath back she wanted to test the theory. If nothing else was to come of their time together other than making her feel good, she could live with it. As long as he didn't break her heart when he tired of being her mentor.

For now she was content to lie in his arms and pretend this feeling of complete and utter bliss was for keeps.

CHAPTER NINE

HENRI DIDN'T THINK he'd ever tire of kissing Lola. Almost a month into their fling, the flames of passion were burning so bright he was in danger of getting burned. It was a shame they'd wasted time avoiding their attraction—now they only had days left before it all ended. Suddenly time was moving way too fast. They needed to make every moment count.

He pressed his lips against hers once more, trying to coax her awake. These mornings waking up with a naked Lola curled up around him were the best way to start the day. He wasn't looking forward to starting night shifts, or to the day when she wouldn't be in his bed at all. Despite their agreement that this was a temporary arrangement, Lola had become part of his life—part of him. He was falling for her—hard—and he didn't know what to do about it.

Having already fallen into a pattern of going to work together when they could, and spending the nights in his bed, they were living as a couple. Even if they hadn't admitted that to anyone—including themselves. He'd never been in love before. He'd seen the havoc it had wreaked in Angelique's life and had always had that in mind when his relationships threatened to get serious. He couldn't afford to be weakened by such a destructive force when the whole family was still dealing with the fallout from the last attack.

Now he was starting to wonder if this was it, and love had sneaked in wearing a pink stethoscope around its neck. This terror taking hold of his heart at the thought of Lola walking away and him never seeing her again was new to him, but he wasn't convinced it could be any worse than the pain when everything crashed and burned. He had no future to offer her. He was tied to helping Angelique raise the children, and Lola would eventually realise she deserved more than last place in the pecking order.

And if Henri was tempted to give in to the whimsy he only had to think of his sister, who'd given herself completely to another, followed him to another country, borne him children and still been left in pieces. Love was messy and complicated and he'd do better without it.

'Hmm…?' Lola's moan in his ear meant they were both stirring.

'Morning.' He turned onto his side so he could stop overthinking this and get lost in the beauty of her yawning smile and still sleepy eyes.

'What am I going to tell Jules this time?'

Lola stretched out her limbs, then cuddled back into Henri's side. A far cry from that first night when she'd stayed over and then panicked about getting home before her absence was noticed—and another indication that they were becoming way too comfortable with the situation.

'You were abducted by aliens and spent the night on board the mother ship?'

'I think I used that one on Tuesday. And if I say I was with my folks again she'll wonder why I ever bothered moving out.'

'You don't think she's the tiniest bit suspicious that something's going on?'

A change in behaviour was always going to draw attention from those who knew them best. Henri had been dodging questions himself about the nature of their relationship—from his sister. But if they admitted they were involved it made it real—and why cause a fuss when it was all but over?

'I think she's too caught up in her own misadventures to notice anything. Besides, Jules isn't the type to hold back. If she thought I was getting it on with a colleague she'd be knocking on the door right now, waiting to hear all the juicy details.'

Lola slid her hand over Henri's chest, apparently ready to give her flatmate something to gossip about. He wasn't complaining. If Lola wasn't in a hurry to bring this out into the open, either, then he was worrying over nothing. After all, she hadn't expressed any desire to extend the parameters of their contract. For now it was only *his* heart at stake.

'You're not in any rush to leave, then?'

'None whatsoever.'

The wicked glint in Lola's eye as she hooked her bare leg around his waist ensured Henri was wide awake and ready to play. Her newfound confidence in the bedroom was a gift to them both and not one to be wasted.

Everything outside of the bedroom door could wait until he was forced to confront it.

'We have an unidentified male in his twenties. Witnesses said he was standing at a bus stop talking on his phone when an assailant punched him in the face and stole it from him. He was knocked unconscious and fell back, cracking his head on the pavement. He hasn't regained consciousness and has been vomiting.'

The paramedic went on to rhyme off his stats and observations while the resus team went to work, trying to get the patient stabilised.

It was Lola's job to suction away the vomit and clear his

airways. It was a task she frequently carried out without a second thought, but at present one which she was finding difficult not to balk at. She put it down to the nerves bubbling inside her, knowing that today was the day she had to have a talk with Henri about their future. One in which, whether he liked it or not, they were now inextricably linked.

Her stomach heaved again. She'd been so incredibly stupid, and there were not enough tears or worry in the world to fix it.

'We're going to need a CT scan and possibly a chest X-ray. I don't think we should try and wake him up, given the possible neurological problems. I'll put in a call to the neuro surgeon and we'll get him moved as soon as we can.'

As ever, Henri was doing everything he could to prevent the worst possible outcome. He could always be counted on to do the right thing. That thought was the only thing getting her through the day without having a nervous breakdown. Henri would know what to do.

Lola just couldn't bear to see the disappointment back in his eyes when she told him what had happened.

A baby. All her hard work to get here and she'd ruined her career in a moment of madness. She was supposed to be leaving the department in a matter of days—the whole point of placements was to learn and move on. How could she do that now with a permanent reminder of her time in A&E and no chance of completing her training?

It must have happened that first night at Henri's. It was the only time they hadn't used protection, and she'd been so carried away by the idea of their fling she hadn't considered the consequences. Brief encounters weren't supposed to end in creating new life. She couldn't even do *that* right.

This was going to change everything—and, from where she was standing, not for the better. When Jules had offered her a room in her apartment neither of them had expected to be sharing with the screaming, pooping product of Lola's illicit affair with their registrar. She was going to have to move out, for a start. And go where? Back home?

If she was worried about Henri's reaction to the news it would be nothing compared to the outrage of her brothers. But what choice would she have as a newly qualified doctor on maternity leave?

Getting knocked up by her superior on her first placement hadn't been part of her life plan. There was no question that she'd wanted something with Henri that lasted beyond her six weeks on his department, but not like this. A pregnancy should evolve from a loving, lasting relationship. Not be an accident which was going to force them to be together.

She wouldn't blame him if he ended up hating her—he hadn't signed on for this, either. But the deed was done and there was a baby on the way. If nothing else he had the right to know he was going to be a father. Now it was all about finding the right place and time to break the news to him gently.

Lola set aside her personal issues to accompany Henri and their patient to the CT scan, waiting silently by his side as images appeared on the screen.

'That's a nasty injury. There are major frontal contusions and serious swelling.' Henri tapped his pen on the screen to point them out, but they were plain to see.

'So they'll operate to relieve the pressure on the brain?'

Perhaps the mothering instinct was kicking in already, but Lola could feel tears welling in her eyes as she stared at the screen. An unnecessary, needless act of violence could end this young man's life before it had barely begun, and *she* was stressing about entering into the next phase of hers.

'He's going to Theatre now, so the neuro surgeons can work on him. They might need to remove part of his skull, and there's a chance of permanent damage, but we've done all we can for now.'

Henri was preparing for the worst, but Lola was still praying he'd pull through.

'Did we find out who he is yet?' she asked, once they'd left the claustrophobic scanning area. He was someone's son...possibly someone's brother.

'The police are still on it.'

'I hope they track down his family. He shouldn't be on his own.'

It could have been one of *her* brothers lying there. Moments like this illustrated how important loved ones were. When she was old and grey and on her deathbed, she imagined an even bigger family around her. One of her own. One which included Henri.

'They will. There are officers here, going through his belongings—it won't be long before they find a contact.'

Henri dropped an unexpected kiss on her head. It wasn't like him to show her any affection at work, when they'd been so careful to keep their affair a secret. An ember of hope flickered to life inside Lola. If he wasn't ready to let her go they might actually be able to salvage something from this mess.

'Fingers crossed. I'm sure they would want to be here with him.'

'*Ma chérie*...always thinking of others.'

Henri stroked her hair back from her face, tucking the wayward strands from her ponytail behind her ear. Lola turned her cheek into his palm and closed her eyes. Nothing else seemed to matter when she was wrapped up in his warmth, and she wished this feeling could last.

The words she needed to say hovered on the tip of her tongue. But the swish of the double doors opening brought the tender moment to an end and forced her to swallow her confession back down.

She backed away, maintaining the illusion of platonic friendship for anyone who passed by. At least by the time her pregnancy started to show she'd be long gone from the department, taking the scandal and her last connection to Henri with her.

That first day seemed a lifetime ago. In a lot of ways it was. Lola wasn't that same timid girl who'd desperately tried to hide from the registrar's view. Now she was a practising doctor, a lover and soon-to-be mother. Neither role was she ready to give up.

Whilst she was coming to terms with the idea of having this baby, she didn't want it to be at the expense of her career, or her relationship with Henri. She wished there was some way she could have it all.

The sadness which had been stalking her since she'd stared at those two blue lines on the pregnancy test finally caught up with her and escaped on a cry.

Henri pulled her into an empty side room and closed the door, obviously still able to compartmentalise all the areas of his life when everything in hers had merged into one.

'Hey, now…I know what you're thinking, but it's not one of your brothers lying there. We've done everything we can and his family will get here—don't worry.'

'It's all so *unfair*.' She hiccuped on another sob, her misery compounded by the fact that Henri assumed her tears were solely for the young man battling for survival. Although hers wasn't a life-or-death situation, everything was hanging in the balance for her, too.

She had to tell him. It was time for her to be brave and face up to whatever fate had in store for her next.

'I know, *chérie*, but I do have some good news for you. Gabrielle came to us last night and told us everything that's been going on with her at school. We've arranged a meeting with her teachers and the parents of the girls involved. It's all very civilised—no shouting, no angry mob with pitchforks—you'd be very proud.'

The worry lines that had accompanied every conversation Henri had had with her about his niece since they'd met had finally evened out. She hated to be the one to put them back.

'I'm so glad for all of you.' There *was* some relief to discover that Gabrielle had finally reached the stage when she was able to confide her troubles in someone other than Lola. Now not only could the school take some action against the bullying, but it also cut the number of secrets Lola was keeping from Henri to one.

'I'm not happy about what she's suffered, but at least we can start to do something about it now. You were right—I don't mind admitting it. There were no dramatics, maybe a few tears, and it all came out on Gabrielle's terms when she was ready. Thanks in no small part to you, she's really started to come out of her shell recently.'

'I don't know…I think her mum and her very understanding uncle had a lot to do with it, too.'

It was a weight off Lola's mind to know that the girl would finally get the help she needed, no matter how it came about. Henri was doing a good job keeping on top of his emotions, too, since no bullies had so far been harmed in the wake of Gabrielle's disclosure. It boded well for the next round of *Did You Know?* that they were yet to play.

'This parenting stuff is stressful. I admire anyone who can juggle it and a career at the same time.'

Henri was giving her the perfect opening. She knew he had respect for his sister, who managed to do both. And it wasn't as if she was asking him to pick one over the other. At this moment she wasn't expecting anything from him except to hear her out.

'It's all good experience for when you have children

of your own. You'll take teenage angst and junk-food-obsessed six-year-olds in your stride by then.'

Lola attempted to steer him towards the role he'd have in another eight months. He'd had plenty of parenting practice over the years, and although it would be a shock, he'd shown himself to be decent father material. It was an attractive quality—even to a non-pregnant bystander.

Unfortunately the snort of derision he gave rendered it a moot point. 'One family is *more* than enough for me.'

'Are you saying you don't want kids of your own some day?'

Lola's heart splintered into a few more pieces. Despite all the impracticalities they would have to overcome, she'd been clinging to the smallest hope that they could somehow make a future together. Now he'd ruled himself out of the loving family she'd imagined around her in that deathbed scene.

'Although my parents didn't intentionally leave us, I feel the same sense of abandonment as Gabrielle and Bastien. I have no intention of extending the legacy. How could I ever be an attentive father to anyone when every minute of my time is accounted for elsewhere? I have a responsibility to Angelique and the children, and I *won't* be another one to walk out on them.'

It was an admirable speech, with Henri making it clear there was no room in his life for anyone else—including Lola. She wanted everything he was telling her he couldn't give her. The fairy tale was coming to an end—without the happy-ever-after she'd longed for.

'I'm sure Angelique wouldn't want you to sacrifice your own happiness on her account.'

Lola couldn't decide if Henri was being completely altruistic or incredibly selfish in his loyalties. She'd endured the crummy childhood and fractured relationships, too, and it had only served to make her desire to create a loving environment for this baby even stronger. Saying he was committed elsewhere was an easy way to avoid admitting he had feelings for anyone other than his family.

Tough. She was going to make him tell her once and for all what she meant to him, and if he wasn't interested she would do this on her own. Lord knew she'd overcome worse problems than having a helpless baby depend on her.

'No, but like my sister, I know my own mind—and nothing is going to change it. Now, enough of the serious stuff. Let's talk cake. Gabrielle's signed up for the local swim team, so she can't make tonight's home baking session.'

Lola's head was spinning and her thoughts were jumbled, piling on top of one another until she was sure her skull would explode with the pressure building up inside. She needed him to shut up so she could think straight.

'I'm pregnant, Henri.'

Suddenly the room was too quiet.

Henri must have misheard. He'd thought she'd said she was pregnant.

'I said I'm pregnant.'

There it was again. The pair of watery green eyes staring at him held no trace of humour.

The bottom of Henri's world plummeted through the floor.

He loosened his tie and gulped in some much needed oxygen. *A baby?* He was always so careful, so responsible, so terrified of this ever happening.

'How? When?'

Lola's tears dried up with her frown. 'I hope you don't expect me to draw you a diagram of how it happened—I'm pretty sure you were there at the time. As for the when... it must've been that first time...you know...we were kind of in a hurry.'

He cast his mind back to that day, when they'd practically thrown Angelique and the kids from the moving car in their haste to get back to his house and consummate their relationship. They hadn't used a condom, but since Lola had never voiced any concern, he'd assumed she was protected.

'Aren't you on the pill?'

'No. Don't start blaming me, Henri. We both messed up.'

'If you'd told me we could have prevented this whole sorry mess with one little pill the next morning.'

Now everything was ruined. Never mind the professional disgrace of getting one of his junior staff pregnant, there was the impact it was going to have on the rest of his family. He'd spent the last ten minutes telling Lola exactly why he didn't want children of his own. For him to turn his back on Angelique and the children now, to support a family he didn't want, simply wouldn't be fair. Fate was playing a desperately cruel joke.

'Do you think I planned this? I'm only weeks into a career I've been studying for years to make a success, living off the goodwill of my flatmate and pregnant by a man who only wanted me in his life for six weeks. It's not the stuff of fairy tales, is it?'

Lola put up a very good argument, but she would have support from her brothers and her friends to get through this. She could go back to work after the baby was born and he would make sure she was financially secure in the meantime. Whereas Henri was the one people turned to in their hour of need—he had no one to do the same for him.

'Who can fathom what goes on in that head of yours? Perhaps you saw me as a safe option? You knew I would never shirk my responsibilities for a child, and I earn enough money to support a woman who can't handle the career she's chosen. I'm the one man you knew wouldn't hurt you.'

'In which case I was sadly mistaken. I'm not asking you for anything, Henri. I simply thought you should know what's happened. Now, if you'll excuse me, I have to at least keep up the pretence that I can do my job until my baby daddy buys me out of it.'

Although Lola's voice had lowered to a gravelly whisper, it was more powerful than if she'd punched him in the place where all this trouble had stemmed from.

Damn it! Deep down Henri knew this wasn't her fault, but the outcome was the same whether she'd planned his downfall or not. He was trapped by circumstance and stupidity with absolutely no chance of escape. This fun, no-strings, short-term thing had suddenly become a lifelong commitment.

He opened his top button, whipped the tie from around his neck. *Breathe in. Breathe out.*

This was the only time he'd actually sympathised with his ex-brother-in-law and understood a fraction of the reason he'd run away. This overwhelming, suffocating sense of responsibility was as close to a panic attack as he'd ever wish to get. His lungs were heaving with every shallow breath, his heart was racing and sweat was breaking over his skin. If he didn't get this under control he'd pass out.

Although unconsciousness was preferable to his current mental state. A few minutes of complete oblivion might be nice, until he got used to the idea that he was going to be a father.

It would be easy to shake everything off and disappear— pretend Lola had never happened. But the difference between Henri and Sean was that *he* was an adult—not a man-child who'd happily let the woman in his life struggle on without any help. Henri had stepped up to the plate when he'd been able to, supporting Angelique financially and emotionally as she'd done for him. Now he'd ruined another woman's life.

He girded his shoulders for another load of guilt to be added to his burden. Although he'd do what he could, he'd let both Lola and Angelique down. Even if he couldn't give either the commitment they deserved, he'd die trying to help.

CHAPTER TEN

LOLA BARELY MADE it through the rest of her shift without emotionally imploding. The one saving grace of the day was hearing that after six hours in surgery the young male with the head injury had pulled through. His family were at his bedside, waiting for him to come round. There was a long road ahead of him but he'd made it this far against the odds.

Only the fear that she'd never stop crying if she started, and the determination to prove she could do anything she put her mind to, had stemmed the flood of tears and prevented her from drowning. Of course the news of impending parenthood was always going to come as a surprise to Henri, but she hadn't expected the slap in the face of his denial. The lovely, caring, child-friendly registrar she'd fallen for had turned out to be just another man capable of inflicting pain.

She'd had more time to get used to the idea—a whole extra twenty-four hours—but at no stage had she pointed the finger of blame. It didn't achieve anything except perhaps shifting responsibility entirely onto her. There was a baby on the way and it would be wanted and loved by at least one parent.

Lola rubbed her still flat belly and imagined the tiny person growing inside who'd caused all the trouble. This mightn't have been the introduction to motherhood she'd planned but, ready or not, it was happening. In a matter of months she'd have a little bundle of her and Henri's genes in her arms. One more to add to clan Roberts.

It was still early days, and there was no need for her pregnancy to disrupt the status quo just yet. She'd tell everyone when she was in the safe zone. Preferably when she was in labour and too high on gas and air to care what they said. For now it was best simply to carry on as normal, with a broken heart and a baby from a relationship no one knew about.

She turned the key in the lock slowly, trying to sneak into the apartment without Jules hearing her. In the privacy of her own room she'd be free to cry and wallow as much as she wanted, without fear of judgement or ridicule. Jules had warned her about the devastating effect the handsome French registrar had on newbies, and now she was paying the ultimate price. She couldn't face *I told you so* on top of everything else.

'Lola—is that you?'

She'd only made it as far as the hall before Jules sprang her.

'Yeah…'

'Well, hello, stranger. What brings you home?'

'I'm not feeling too well. I think I'll have an early night.' Lola hustled towards the bedroom—only to find a Jules-shaped obstacle in her path.

'Don't tell me your secret lover is otherwise engaged tonight? I thought you two were joined at the hip.'

'Wh—what?' Lola stuttered, racking her brain for a better cover story. Apparently she wasn't the expert at keeping secrets she'd thought she was.

'You didn't *really* expect me to buy that rubbish about staying with the family when you were so desperate to get away from them in the first place? Besides, you've been wearing that cat-got-the-cream smile that only comes from great sex. *I* should know. It's been killing me, waiting until you were ready to tell me. Patience never was my strongpoint, and since I have no gossip of my own it's only fair I get to hear yours.'

Jules widened her stance and folded her arms, trapping Lola in the small corridor so she couldn't outrun her lies. This was the same kind of pressure *she'd* put on Gabrielle when she'd been tasked with extracting her troubles. She'd forgotten that finally voicing your worries also released the emotions bottled up alongside them. The final barrier gave way and a torrent of sorrow began to pour down Lola's face before she even got to confirm Jules's suspicion.

'Oh, my God, Lola—what's wrong?' Jules immediately wrapped her arms around her and let her cry her heart out.

Lola was sure that was literally what she'd done. All that was left when she stopped was an empty space in her chest where Henri had once resided.

It only hurt because she cared for him so much. Regardless of all the warnings her heart and head had given out, she'd fallen for him during those glorious hours in his bed, discovering everything about him, and herself.

'I...' She choked, unable to find the beginning of her sorry tale. So much good had come from her tryst with Henri it seemed a shame to erase it and focus on the bitter ending.

'Come and sit down and I'll get you a glass of water. Do we need cookies, too?'

Jules manoeuvred her towards the kitchen and into a chair. However, no amount of cupcakes or cookies could fix this one. Although she'd usually eat her feelings away, her appetite had vanished along with her periods.

After a lot of banging about, Jules returned with two glasses and a bottle of wine. 'I thought this might require something stronger.'

Lola considered drinking herself into a stupor for a split second—before her subconscious piped up to remind her that her body was no longer hers alone. She promptly erupted into another bout of weeping.

The glasses clinked beside her as Jules set them down to comfort her again. 'You're scaring me now. All I did was offer you a drink—'

Lola gave her non-existent bump a fleeting glance, but it was enough to make her friend gasp in horror.

'You're not…?'

What could she do but nod her head? 'I'm pregnant.'

Jules collapsed into the chair beside her and grabbed her hand. 'Oh, sweetheart. Who's the father? Scrub that. It doesn't matter. I take it he's not interested, or you wouldn't be in such a state. Don't you worry. We'll get through this together.'

'Thanks…' Lola mumbled into her BFF's cleavage as she was swamped in another hug.

This was the reaction she'd wanted from Henri—a promise that everything would be all right, not resentment and blame. Losing Henri was the most upsetting aspect of all this for her—not the prospect of having his baby. She'd wanted him to love her as much as she loved him.

'What do you want me to do? Run you a bath? Make you a cuppa? Tell me what I can do to make this better for you? Give me the word and I'll hunt down the scumbag who's done this to you and make sure he's not capable of doing it again.'

The idea of Jules turning up on Henri's doorstep brandishing her stilettos as lethal weapons appealed to Lola's warped sense of humour. He deserved to feel as frightened as she was, but there was no need to burn all her bridges. When the dust settled they would have to have some sort of grown-up conversation about their child and Henri's involvement in its life—if any.

'Thanks for the offer. I might take you up on it some time. To be honest, I think I need to clear my head. I could do with some fresh air.'

'Whatever you need.'

What she needed was for Henri to be the one to put his arms around her and tell her everything was okay. Instead she set off outside into the night with no clue where she was going. She didn't know how or why, but she found herself walking into Angelique's burlesque class. Perhaps it was because it was the one place she'd ever really been free to be herself before Henri came along.

'Lola! I'm so glad you came.' Angelique, dressed in nothing but feathers and sequins, greeted her with a double cheek-kiss.

'I haven't booked or anything. If there's no space I can come back another time.' Lola could see there were already a few excitable women present, including a lively hen party. She'd made a mistake in coming here on her own, without Jules to chivvy her along.

'Not at all. We'd love another body—wouldn't we girls?'

Angelique took over the pushy-friend role, ensuring she joined the whooping women and became part of their strange dancing troupe.

'Now, I thought we'd do something special for the occasion. Most of you have been here before and learnt the basics. So why don't we put it into practice on the stage... for your stags?'

Angelique clapped and a small band of jeering men walked out onto the dance floor. The women were equally raucous at seeing their counterparts, and Lola imagined they'd stopped off in a few pubs before they'd brought the party here.

Lola held up her hand. 'That's me out.'

Dancing on stage for the entertainment of a group of inebriated letches wouldn't help her mood one iota. Besides, they wouldn't miss an ugly duckling like her slinking away, when there were so many bright and beautiful birds willing to shake their tail feathers.

'Where do you think *you're* going?' Hands on hips, Angelique did the best impression of a strict school headmistress she could manage in her frou-frou outfit.

'It's a step too far for me I'm afraid. Thanks, Angelique, but I think I'll head home.'

All she'd wanted was space to forget—not to have another bunch of men wheeled in to heap more humiliation on her and add to this day from hell.

'Hey, I get that this is a big step, but if it's confidence you're working on then this is exactly what you need. Do you think *I* wasn't nervous about sharing the stage with girls half my age in Paris? You bet your ass I was. But I did it, and it was the best thing I've ever done. I didn't care who was looking at me—it was enough to know I was there, dancing for myself and no one else. Tonight was the bridesmaids' idea, and these guys are all taken. I'll keep them in line, so you'll have no worries on that score. My advice is to get up and do this for yourself.'

Angelique delivered her motivational speech and walked away, leaving Lola to make her own decision on the subject.

She looked again at the crowd behind her. Certainly the stags and hens had paired off, with eyes only for each other. A couple of other unattached ladies chatted excitedly, apparently none of them experiencing the same level of anxiety she had as she anticipated dancing up there.

She moved quietly towards the stage without anyone taking any notice. There was nothing special about the area itself—no spotlights or dazzling effects to make it any more remarkable than a raised platform. Lola supposed it was more about what it represented that frightened her. This was where they were supposed to show off, and she'd gained a lot more than dancing skills since attending the class.

In another few months her body would change beyond all recognition. This could be her last chance to do this. Especially when the news broke about her pregnancy and her friendship with Angelique changed irrevocably.

The only other time she'd been on show for a baying crowd had changed her life for ever. Maybe this time she could make it for the better. The prospect of being a single parent left no room for insecurities. She would have to lead by example if she was going to raise her child to be a warrior rather than a victim. Although if she did this it would be her choice—and she most certainly wouldn't be naked.

'Do you have any costumes?'

Angelique clapped her hands together and gave a squeal. 'Do *I* have *costumes*? That's akin to asking the Queen if she has any hats.'

The Queen of the dance hall wheeled out a rainbow of sparkling corsets and accessories, and soon Lola was marvelling at the exquisite embroidery and daring styles on the rail.

'These are beautiful.'

'Does this mean you've turned to the dark side?' Angelique held an electric blue silk ensemble in front of Lola.

'I'm not sure it's my colour…' But Lola thought it might be worthwhile trying it on anyway.

Most of the girls went for the more risqué options—cleavage-enhancing, thigh-exposing outfits guaranteed to make an impression on the now seated audience. Lola on the other hand, chose a more modest pearly pink corset with matching frilly skirt. The girly princess style was more her than the vampy red and black siren suits, but it didn't stop her shaking with nerves, knowing that her lady bits were covered only with layers of chiffon and silk.

From the wings, wrapped in the stage curtain, Lola

watched as the others took to the stage one by one. The response so far had been very positive, with dancers and spectators alike smiling and enjoying themselves. A few girls had even stripped off their stockings and gloves to throw to their admirers. There were no rules—no right and wrong ways to dance. It was all about letting go and celebrating their bodies.

For Lola, it was also about embracing her pregnancy and moving into the next chapter of her life.

Suddenly Lola was the last showgirl standing. Shaking. Panicking. And liable to vomit all over her bespoke 'coming out' frock.

'Lola?' Angelique gently rested her hand on Lola's shoulder. 'Do you still want to do this?'

'No.' It was an honest answer, but as she saw Angelique head for the stage herself Lola unwrapped herself from the curtain and stopped her. 'But I *need* to do this.'

For the first few bars of the song Lola couldn't move. She closed her eyes, let the sultry music wash over her and stepped out of her hiding place. The audience was a blur at the corner of her eye as she wiggled her way across the stage. She didn't dare look directly at them in case her wobbly legs gave way altogether. Then she really would make a spectacle of herself—and flash parts of her she was determined to keep secret in public.

There were a few wolf whistles as she stroked the full length of her black silk gloves, a chorus of cheers as she moved her hands down her body to rest them on her lap. Once she realised she wasn't going to be booed off she started to relax. She dipped to her knees and swivelled around, giving her booty a pop as she straightened again. With one foot crossed in front of the other, she sashayed to the back of the stage. She raised her arms above her head with a flourish, and slowly slid them back down to stroke her face in profile.

A salsa move forwards and back, combined with a turn, brought her to face her nightmare. There was no one laughing behind their hand at her attempts to dance, so she took that as a positive and carried on. It was all about revelling in her own body, touching every part of her as only a lover could. She stroked her fingers across her chest, dipped her hand between her legs and parted her thighs in a quick flash. It was empowering to say *You can look but not touch* as she bounced back up into a body roll.

Angelique had called it. This was more about knowing she *could* do it if she chose and nothing to do with content. Perhaps she could get the hospital trust to introduce corset and stockings as the new uniform as she was now so comfortable in it?

She kicked her leg out to the side and slowly teased her hand to the top of her stocking, her head thrown back in mock ecstasy. It only worked for real when there was a Frenchman inching along her thigh.

The faces of those pimply teens who'd made her ashamed of her own body faded with every body-pop and wiggle of her hips, until she was drained of all her energy. She'd done what she'd come up here to do and she wanted to finish on a high. With a sidestep, she bent over at the waist and gave a shimmy.

Lola Roberts was finally flaunting what God gave her.

She finished to a round of applause and a surge of adrenaline shooting through her body. For a fleeting moment she thought she saw Henri through her teary eyes. Real or imaginary, he was the one person in the room who *hadn't* enjoyed her performance.

Henri wished he'd never come. The sight of Lola performing up there only added a sense of urgency to the problem he'd come to discuss with his sister. He'd come for advice—not a reminder of what he'd thrown away.

Lola was blossoming before his very eyes. He only had to see her peacocking in one of Angelique's outfits to know how far she'd come from the girl who'd hated anyone looking at her. More than that, her confidence in her own abilities at work was growing every day, too. She'd jumped in today to help with that trauma patient without any coaxing from him.

It wasn't jealousy that consumed Henri as he watched her strut fearlessly in her costume, it was pride. At a time when she should be devastated about stalling her career she was owning this new side of her—living up to her showgirl namesake. The sparkle was back in her eyes as she mingled on the dance floor with the others, her head held high with every step she took in her stripper heels.

He walked away, realising he was superfluous to her requirements. While she'd left her baggage up on that stage, Henri was still trailing his behind him.

Today had made him question every aspect of his connection with Lola. He'd been unforgivably selfish and stupid for lashing out at her when it was himself he was angry at. It wasn't *her* fault he'd done the unthinkable and fallen in love with her. He'd already been afraid to tell her how much she meant to him when he was juggling his guilt and his responsibilities to Angelique. The revelation that there was a baby on the way had forced him to face those feelings and he'd reacted like a caged animal—attacking first before he got hurt.

They hadn't ever discussed carrying on their fling after Lola's placement ended. For all he knew she resented him for getting her pregnant, ruining her career and tying her to him for the rest of her days. But he loved Lola, and he'd nearly destroyed her because of it.

He sat in the front seat of his car, trying to make sense of the chaos he'd created. It wasn't fair to judge his relationship with Lola on the basis of the debt he owed to his sister. If he took Angelique and the children out of the equation, what was he left with? A woman he loved and wanted to be with and a baby borne of that union. It seemed so simple when he stripped away the layers of guilt and pig-headedness.

Above all, he wanted to be with her. Everything else would simply have to fit in around that. As long as she wanted him, too.

CHAPTER ELEVEN

LOLA DIDN'T KNOW how she was managing to function at work, but she wouldn't give Henri the satisfaction and phone in sick just so she wouldn't have to face him. To say she was devastated at his rejection was an understatement. Her tear-drenched pillow and the stockpile of brownies in the kitchen would attest to that. Perhaps she'd had a lucky escape from someone who would accuse her of getting pregnant to keep him, but it would take some time to see it that way. For now she was still pretty bruised.

She stepped into the cubicle to check on her next patient, an eighty-year-old woman who'd been admitted with breathing difficulties.

'Hello, Vera. Can you tell me where the pain is?'

The nursing staff had already made her as comfortable as possible, sitting her up to aid her breathing and attaching an oxygen mask.

'It's in my back.'

'And can you tell me—is it the pain or the breathing which is worse?' Lola could see from her notes that she'd fallen, and there could be confusion between her internal and external injuries.

'The breathing…' Vera stuttered out from behind the mask.

'I'm just going to listen to your chest, okay?'

Lola unhooked her stethoscope from around her neck and pressed it against the old lady's skin. She could hear the bubbling sound of fluid in the air sacs of the lungs—a definite sign of something more serious than a chest infection. Lola tapped on her chest and the dull thud replacing what should have been a hollow, drum-like sound also indicated that fluid could be collecting in between the layers of the lung membrane.

Chest X-rays and blood tests confirmed Lola's suspicion that she was battling pneumonia and that there was fluid there along with infection in the lungs. The poor woman was struggling to breathe, and with her medical history Lola didn't think the prognosis was good. She needed advice from someone who had more experience in this area, but she was appalled to find Henri was today's leading clinician.

Only the welfare of her elderly patient persuaded her to approach him.

'Lola! I'm so glad you—'

'If you have a minute, I'd like a second opinion on one of my patients.' She spread the notes out on the desk in front of him, trying not to brush against him or make eye contact if she could help it.

'Certainly. What have we got?'

He was much too cheery for a man who'd broken her heart only yesterday. If he didn't know the accepted etiquette after breaking up with a pregnant girlfriend was to appear shame-faced and grovelling for forgiveness she might have to remind him with a swift kick. *After* they'd treated the patient.

'An eighty-year-old female with pneumonia. Her breathing is laboured, but she has chronic heart and lung disease. I don't want to put her on a ventilator yet, in case we have difficulty getting her off it again.'

There was a danger she would become too reliant on it and would never manage to breathe on her own again.

'You're right. Continue with the oxygen and antibiotics for now. Her next twenty-four hours will be crucial, but we'll do what we can to help her fight. Try to keep her as calm as possible, because anxiety will only affect her breathing more. Are her family here?'

Henri gathered the notes back into a neat pile and handed them back to Lola. She hated her body for betraying her as his fingers brushed hers. He had no right to still make her tremble with one touch after what he'd done.

'They're on their way.'

'I'll pop over with you and say hello.'

She didn't want to spend any more time with him than was strictly required. These last days were going to drag on if he insisted on torturing her by being near.

'That's really not necessary. I'm sure you have other stuff to do. All I wanted was some advice—and, trust me, if there was anyone else I could've turned to I would have.'

She turned on her heel before he could see how much she'd let him get to her.

'I need to apologise—'

'Yes, you do—but this isn't the time or the place.'

She didn't want to hear a half-hearted explanation of his behaviour dropped into conversation between patients. The least she deserved was a proper discussion about what they were going to do next. In the meantime she had people relying on her, and everything except Vera would have to wait.

'Hi, Vera. We've decided to keep topping up the antibiotics, and as soon as you're feeling a bit better we can move you up on to the ward. Okay?'

It was all about keeping her calm, giving her hope.

Vera nodded, although her eyes were wide with panic.

Lola was concerned she was accepting defeat and giving up the fight.

'*Bonjour.* My name is Henri and I'm the registrar here. I wanted to come and see how you are.'

Lola rolled her eyes as he appeared—in full French mode. She was sure he exaggerated that accent for the effect it had on the ladies. It wouldn't surprise Lola if he actually had a broader Belfast brogue than her and this whole charade was solely to pick up women. Even Vera sat up straighter upon hearing it.

'We're just getting Mrs McConville comfortable until we can move her on to the general ward.' *I've got this.*

'*Très bon.* I've been in touch with your son and daughter and they want to come and see how you're doing.'

He was very calm, and Lola could see he was trying not to spook Vera by telling her of their arrival. It could be overwhelming—frightening, even—when families turned up en masse, weeping and wailing at the bedside.

'Can I get you a wee drink, Vera? Your lips are very dry…' Lola held a cup to her mouth so she could take a sip.

'What do you say I take you for a proper cuppa and some cake when you're feeling better?' Henri asked, and managed to bring a smile to the thin cracked lips behind the oxygen mask.

He did have a way with women of all ages, and it simply didn't fit with the cruelty he'd inflicted on Lola yesterday.

'Now, *that's* an offer and a half, Vera, isn't it? We'll have to get you fighting fit and get that date nailed down.' Lola carried on with the teasing since it was taking the woman's mind off her immediate problem. She was already starting to relax, and her breathing was a lot steadier than when she'd first arrived.

Henri must have noticed, too, and he began to remove Vera's mask. 'I'm just going to take you off the oxygen for a bit. I think the antibiotics are beginning to take effect and I want to see how you do on your own for a while. If you're in pain or struggling let me know and we'll put it back on again. Okay?'

Vera rubbed at her skin, where the straps had left marks, and sighed. 'It's my own fault for going out without a coat or brolly. I wouldn't be here if I hadn't got caught in that rain.'

'We all make mistakes. The important thing is what we do to fix them.'

Henri stared meaningfully at Lola, and it was all she could do not to reach across the bed and slap him. Was he really suggesting they should 'fix' her pregnancy? He sank even lower in her estimation.

'These things happen, but we can't beat ourselves up over them, Vera. Sometimes we've just got to man up and deal with it. We've got to have faith that everything will come good in the end.' Lola smiled brightly at Vera and hooked her chart over the end of the bed. All the while shooting invisible daggers in Henri's direction.

'And sometimes we overreact when we realise we've screwed up. Mistakes can turn out to be the best thing that's ever happened to us, only we're too stupid to see it at first.'

He deflected Lola's imaginary flying weapons with a smouldering look she didn't think was meant for their pensioner. Lola tried to ignore her overexcited internal organs as they went into overdrive. Although this had the markings of an apology, there was no guarantee anything would change between them. He was probably just trying to save face in front of Vera.

The woman lying between them turned her head, following their conversation back and forth as though she was at a tennis match. 'Have you two had a falling out?'

'No.'

'Yes.'

Henri apparently thought it was safer to have this out in front of an audience. But if this was his way of getting around her without a fight it wasn't going to work.

'Oh, dear. Has he been playing away, love? They're famous for that, the French, aren't they?'

Vera settled herself down for a good gossip and it might have been comical if this wasn't Lola's *life* playing out in the middle of the emergency department.

'Not that I know of.'

'No, but I did do something else unforgivable.'

Henri immediately allayed the fear that there might be another reason he didn't want to commit before it had a chance to form fully in Lola's worry bank.

'Has he apologised?' Vera's arms were folded, and her lips pursed as she planted herself firmly in Lola's camp.

'Sort of.'

Henri cleared his throat. 'That's what I'm trying to do now.'

Vera narrowed her eyes at him. 'You're not doing a very good job of it. You should be down on bended knee, begging for her forgiveness. I thought you lot were supposed to be experts at sweeping women off their feet? Make him *work* for it, Doctor.'

It wasn't often Henri who was the one taking orders rather than giving them, and Lola enjoyed watching him squirm at the bedside, trying to decide if he should actually get down on the floor.

'That's really not necessary, Mrs McConville. I wouldn't expect Dr Benoit to make such a gesture in public. I'm his dirty little secret.'

Lola left with a wink, trusting her new best friend to give Henri the pasting he deserved for treating her so appallingly while she organised a porter to move her patient to the general ward.

Lola didn't want to be part of a pantomime played out

so Henri could salve his conscience. Even if he'd finally decided he would play a part in the baby's life it would never be enough. There was a 'buy one get one free' deal going here, and despite everything she still wanted him to take up the offer.

Otherwise it was going to kill her, being so close to the man she loved every day and getting nothing in return. She was thinking seriously about asking for a transfer before the end of her placement.

'Give me a break, Vera. I tried.'

Henri was still getting the stink-eye from Lola's bed-bound cheerleader. This wasn't easy for him. He could count on one hand the number of times he'd had to apologise in his life and for it to carry so much importance. Every time the words formed in his head he looked at Lola and nothing seemed adequate to portray the depth of his emotions for her.

He would have crawled on his hands and knees if he'd thought it would make any difference, but he could sense those walls already forming around Lola again—and he'd been the architect.

'If you love her you'll do more than try, you eejit.'

This indomitable spirit would serve the old lady well. Hopefully she would be back on her feet once the infection had cleared. Lola had made a difficult decision in keeping her off the ventilator at the first sign of her breathing difficulties, but it had worked out in the end. With the amount of problems Vera had going on already it would have been too easy for her body to give up altogether. This way she at least had a fighting chance.

'Let's get you sorted out first.'

He made way for the porter at the bedside, making sure Vera was comfortable before they moved her.

'I'm going, I'm going,' he said, in response to another glower.

Vera lifted her hand to wave at him as she was wheeled out of the department. She was a fighter, putting cowardly men who gave up at the first hint of trouble to shame. It was time he took a stand for something he wanted, *needed* from life.

He'd never known how to live for himself without always being mindful of how it would impact on his family. It was an exciting, if daunting prospect. Made worse with the knowledge that he'd given up a future with Lola when no one had asked him to. He'd jumped ahead, skipping the part where they could have had something meaningful, anticipating the reasons why it would never work.

He chased Lola down through the corridors. 'I'm an eejit, according to Vera.'

Her footsteps faltered and she spoke without turning to look at him. 'Yes. What's your point?'

'I thought I would be doing wrong by my family in spending more time with you. You don't understand… Angelique gave up everything to raise me after our parents died. How do you ever repay *that*? Well, I thought it was my duty to be there for her and the kids—make the same sacrifice she had made for me. She walked away from the very thing she loved to make sure I had a better life. I thought I had to do the same.'

The time, money and the other relationships he'd given up to atone were small gestures compared to the great loss he'd suffered at his own hand. Couldn't she see that?

'I don't think I would've wanted a three-way relationship anyway. What woman wants to be in competition with a man's *sister* for his affections? Badly done or not, this is for the best.'

She took another step forwards.

'But that's it. I was wrong. Angelique is perfectly capable of managing on her own—she doesn't need me. No one needs me. But I need *you*. I love you, Lola.'

His voice cracked as he said it and the implications of the words hit him. He'd never said that to anyone—not even his beloved sister. When he'd lost his parents he'd stopped believing love had any purpose other than bringing pain to those involved. That was still true now. But above all else Lola had to know that someone cared about her. Even if he was a complete imbecile who wasn't worthy of her.

'Maybe that's not enough. *I love you* is right up there with *I didn't mean to hurt you*. It's meaningless without the actions to back it up.'

Lola had put him in the same category as every other man who'd used and abused her on a whim. Unfortunately that didn't leave any room for him to make amends.

He stood helpless as Lola denied him redemption and disappeared through the door, but he didn't believe there wasn't still a flicker of hope. Those tears she was trying to hide were too real, too raw for her to be pretending she didn't care about him. It was down to him to give it one last shot and try to make it up to her.

If Lola needed a grand gesture to prove his love to her, she was going to get it.

Lola had no real desire to have another heart-to-heart with Jules about her predicament. She'd had enough of those for one day and had accomplished nothing.

Even hearing Henri say those three little words hadn't had the effect she'd imagined. There had been no choir of angels heralding the hallelujah moment when everything fell into place, because he hadn't yet told her this was for keeps. She'd been bitten twice now, so it was hardly surprising she was reluctant to take another man at face value. Especially since he'd proved he wasn't the man she'd thought he was.

Another temporary placement in his bed wasn't enough any more. She wanted a partner and a father for her baby. There was more than *her* future at stake here.

As she opened the apartment door it struck her that she was becoming very demanding of late, and unwilling to settle for anything less than she deserved. It was ironic that she was finally becoming an independent woman when everything was falling apart. But from now on she would put all her efforts into raising this child and leave all thought of romance where it belonged—in books.

The living room was in darkness, so she assumed Jules wasn't home yet—until she saw candles burning around the room. She dropped her bag on the sofa, to make sure she didn't stumble over it in the dark.

'Did we have a power cut, Jules?'

A shadow rose from the chair opposite and moved into the flickering candlelight. 'No power cut. No Jules. Just me.'

Lola swallowed her drool as Henri made his presence known—all six-foot-whatever dressed in a tux. The soft sound of blues music played in the background, and as her eyes adjusted to the darkness she could see rose petals strewn around the floor. She'd walked into her pre-pregnancy fantasy.

'How did you get in?'

'Jules very kindly lent me her key.'

'You told her about us?'

'I think she figured it out when I begged her to help me woo you.'

'*Woo* me?'

'*Oui*. Woo you.'

That accent slayed her every time.

He took a step closer and Lola resisted the urge to move

back to a place of safety. There was no more running away
from this for either of them.

'How do you propose to do that? Did Vera give you
some more advice when I wasn't looking?'

Lola wasn't impressed with his track record so far. The
last time he'd attempted to seduce her he'd combined it
with babysitting duties and a work conference. He wasn't
as smooth as his reputation led a girl to believe.

'I decided against grovelling on the hospital floor in
favour of a more traditional approach. You danced for me
last night, and I thought you might appreciate a partner
this time.'

He slipped one hand around her waist and laced the fingers of the other hand with hers, leading her in a gentle
waltz to the middle of the living room.

'You *saw* me last night?'

She'd thought she'd imagined him—*and* that look of
disgust as he walked away. She stumbled over her feet, but
Henri pulled her tight against him and carried on dancing.

'You were beautiful—so confident and sexy and carrying *my* baby. I was so proud, watching you up there.'

'Really? I thought you were ashamed of me.' Lola tried
her best not to get carried away by the praise and Henri's acknowledgement of the child they'd created together.
There was no point in getting her hopes up that they could
be a family when her time here was almost up.

'Never. You're part of me, Lola, and I don't want to be
without you ever again. Either of you. Will you marry me?'

He rested his hand on her belly, on their future, and Lola
really wanted to believe it was possible to have everything
she'd ever dreamed of.

'Not so long ago you were blaming me for getting pregnant and extending the time limit on our *arrangement*. I
don't want you to propose because you think it's the right
thing to do. What's happened to change the way you feel

about me, us?' This wasn't going to work if he'd some-how been strong-armed into romancing her. Jules could be lurking in the shadows somewhere pulling the strings and making him dance.

'Nothing has changed my feelings for you. I've been in love with you from the moment I saw you dancing upside down in that chair. I've simply been too afraid to admit it.' Big brave Henri confessing the slightest hint of fear was confirmation enough that this was the real deal.

Lola cast her mind back to that night in the hotel when he'd taken his time with her, understanding exactly what she'd needed. She pictured him today, with her pneumonia patient, going beyond the call of duty to make sure Vera was at ease. Instinct told her that Henri was everything he was selling himself as with this stunt.

'Ask me again.' This time she wanted the moment free from doubts and suspicion.

'Lola Roberts, will you do me the honour of marry-ing me?'

Her battered heart finally waved the white flag. 'Yes, Henri. I will marry you.'

It seemed she wasn't done with testing her bravery just yet.

EPILOGUE

'I HOPE YOU'RE ready for this…' Henri whispered into Lola's ear and stood every hair on the back of her neck to attention. Family get-togethers were all well and good unless you were forced to keep your hands off your sexy fiancé— in which case they were damn frustrating.

'It can't be *that* bad.' Lola carried on setting the table for Sunday lunch, looking forward to an afternoon with Angelique and the children.

'My sister isn't renowned for her cooking—as you well know.' Henri gave a shudder and took his seat at the head of the table.

'I heard that!' Angelique carried in dishes of mashed potato and veg, while Gabrielle proudly followed with a platter of roast beef. 'I just wanted to do something to celebrate your engagement. Besides, Gabs did most of the cooking. All I did was boil the kettle to make the gravy.'

'*You* did this, Gabrielle? That's *amazing*. Well done.'

Lola hadn't seen much of the blushing teenager since she'd taken on a lot of after-school activities—including dance lessons with her mother. There hadn't been any more mention of problems at school, and Lola hoped life was starting to improve for her.

'Thank goodness we have one member of the family

who can cook. I haven't had a decent home-made meal in about twenty years.'

Henri took a healthy scoop from each of the dishes as he sat down, and dodged the Yorkshire pudding Angelique threw at his head. It was the sort of camaraderie Lola had missed with her brothers.

'I should probably look into organising a family dinner at my dad's, too. God knows the last time they ate anything other than takeout, and it's about time I introduced you to them, Henri.'

She casually threw that at him, without referencing the inquisition he'd inevitably endure at the hands of her siblings. For safety's sake she might suggest he wear body armour for the occasion once they found out about her pregnancy.

Henri stopped wolfing down his dinner for long enough to stare. 'You want me to meet your family?'

'It's going to become obvious pretty quickly that something's up, and if I don't tell them about you they'll go into full stalker mode.'

Lola patted the soft swell of her belly under the table. They'd delayed sharing their news until they'd had the three-month scan, to make sure everything was progressing as it should, but she wouldn't be able to hide it much longer. No more secrets, no more lies. She couldn't wait for everyone to share in the good news.

'Wait…have you guys got something to tell us?' Gabrielle's cutlery clattered onto her plate at this revelation.

'Er…' Lola waited for Henri to drop the bombshell. He'd become quite the proud father already, poring over the scan pictures and trying to teach the baby French via her belly button.

'We're going to have a baby.'

He was positively beaming as he extended the Benoit family by another two. Telling them they intended to get married soon, so the baby would naturally take his surname—as would Lola.

There were gasps and happy whoops around the table—except from Bastien, who made an *'Eww!'* sound instead.

'I'm so happy for you both.' Angelique was on her feet at once to hug them, giving Henri an extra squeeze.

There was nothing but love in her embrace, and Lola hoped she and Henri could stop worrying that this would somehow have a negative impact on the family dynamic.

'I'm going to have a cousin!' Gabrielle rushed to kiss Lola, too, and immediately offered her babysitting services for when the time came.

Far from pouting about the prospect of being left out once the new addition arrived, everyone was as excited as the parents-to-be. Lola was lucky to be part of two loving families. She was sure her brothers would be putty in her baby's squidgy little hands, too, once they got used to the idea of their wee sister being pregnant.

'That means *you'll* have someone to boss about, too, Bastien.' Henri extracted a worrying grin from his otherwise unimpressed nephew.

'We have some news of our own to share.' Angelique diverted everyone's attention as she and the children shared knowing looks. 'I'm taking the kids to Paris over the holidays, to show them our old stomping ground and see the sights. It's about time they embraced their French culture, don't you think, Henri?'

'You're going on your own?' He tensed beside Lola, and she could see this would be a real test for him. But he had to let go if they were to stand any chance of making it as a family in their own right.

'Yes, Henri. I'm taking my kids on holiday to spend some quality time with them. Do you have a problem with that?' Her eyes glittered, daring him to challenge her, and there was a heavy air of expectation as they waited for his response.

Henri took a sip of water, rolled his napkin into a ball and rose from his seat. Lola tensed, afraid that everything they'd worked for was about to unravel before her eyes. He'd spent his entire adulthood caring for his sister and her brood, and this was the first time as far as Lola knew that they were striking out on their own. It was a lot for him to get used to.

Henri reached down and kissed Angelique on the cheek. 'I'm sure you'll have a lovely time. Make sure you take plenty of photographs, so I can see what the old place looks like now.'

'I will—but there's nothing to stop you two going to visit yourselves some time. There's nothing like a dirty weekend in Paris…'

Angelique trailed off, as if she was remembering one. It seemed she had some secrets of her own.

'How about it?' Henri asked when they were washing up in the kitchen.

'Hmm?' Lola was distracted by his thick forearms, dipping into the soapy bubbles, clearly visible now he'd rolled his sleeves up.

'I'm talking about Angelique's suggestion of a dirty weekend in Paris. It's the perfect place for a honeymoon.'

Henri encircled her waist with his wet hands and pulled her close. She couldn't remember one good reason why she would want to be anywhere else other than here in his arms.

'Why wait for a honeymoon when our place is only a short drive away?'

Paris could wait. Lola couldn't. She shrieked as Henri took her legs from beneath her and swept her into his arms.

'We have to go, Angelique. There's an emergency. I'll

speak to you tomorrow. Maybe…' Henri yelled his good-byes and carried Lola out to the car with the urgency of a man on a mission.

This time there was no question over his priorities, and Lola couldn't wait to reap the benefits. She was determined to show Henri exactly how much she loved him. Every single day.

* * * * *

MILLS & BOON®

Want to get more from Mills & Boon?

Here's what's available to you if you join the exclusive **Mills & Boon eBook Club** today:

✦ *Convenience – choose your books each month*
✦ *Exclusive – receive your books a month before anywhere else*
✦ *Flexibility – change your subscription at any time*
✦ *Variety – gain access to eBook-only series*
✦ *Value – subscriptions from just £3.99 a month*

So visit **www.millsandboon.co.uk/esubs** today to be a part of this exclusive eBook Club!

MILLS & BOON®

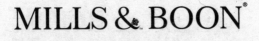

THE ULTIMATE IN ROMANTIC MEDICAL DRAMA

A sneak peek at next month's titles...

In stores from 2nd October 2015:

- **The Baby of Their Dreams** – Carol Marinelli *and*
  Falling for Her Reluctant Sheikh – Amalie Berlin

- **Hot-Shot Doc, Secret Dad** *and*
  Father for Her Newborn Baby – Lynne Marshall

- **His Little Christmas Miracle** – Emily Forbes
- **Safe in the Surgeon's Arms** – Molly Evans
